The Dead Stripper

a Steve Piasecki novel, Volume 1

Barry Bowe

Published by First Clue Publishing, 2022.

This is a work of fiction. Similarities to real people, places, or events are entirely coincidental.

THE DEAD STRIPPER

First edition. March 1, 2022.

Copyright © 2022 Barry Bowe.

ISBN: 979-8201415471

Written by Barry Bowe.

CHAPTER 1

South Philadelphia – March 2018

I'm approaching Geno's Steaks at the intersection of 9th and Passyunk when my cellphone rings. It's 11:09 on a cool spring night. March 7th. A Wednesday.

The phone's mounted in the middle of the dashboard. I look at the caller ID and see **MY FRIEND**. Put the call on speaker. "I see your beater phone's working tonight."

"Ha-ha-ha." My Friend fakes a laugh. "I got a good phone."

My Friend's real name is Mike. He's a wrestler with the East Coast Wrestling Association. Goes by Hit Man Bruno in the ring.

Yes, it's a professional wrestling organization, but these guys do it more for love than money. Some are over the hill, hanging on because they don't want to quit. Others, like My Friend, are still young and hopeful of catching that first big break. But either way, no one's making big bucks. So they work conventional jobs, moonlight, or do both to support their families.

"You Ubering?" My Friend asks.

"Yep. You working?"

"Started an hour ago," My Friend says. "Three stinking pools. Maybe 15 bucks. Not worth the time they take. Before I forget. I'm wrestling Saturday night. Dough Boy pulled a hammy."

—

A tall brunette's entering the employees' coat-room at a topless club.

She's 23, attractive and shapely, goes by Jade. Wearing dangling earrings and a heart-shaped gold necklace. Tan blouse and tight jeans.

She's carrying a makeup case and two large Macy's shopping bags. Places the makeup case on a shelf, sets the bags on the floor. Starts putting on her brown leather jacket.

One of the bouncers creeps up behind her. He's 30, muscular, looks Italian. Tattooed arms complete his menacing look. "Done for the night?"

His voice startles her. She turns to face him. "What's it look like?"

"Need a ride?" he asks.

"No thanks."

"Seriously," he says, "I'll give ya a ride."

"Rather take an Uber."

"Why?"

"Why do you wanta give me a ride?"

"You know," he says. "Like, as a favor."

"Bullshit. You just want me to suck your cock."

"Why the attitude?" he asks. "Thought we had a good thing going."

"We did. Until you fucked Charity."

"That?" he says. "That didn't mean nuthin. Come on. I'll make it up to ya."

"Don't make me laugh. I moved on from you."

"With who?" he asks.

"Nunna your business."

"Gimme one more chance." He moves closer.

"Don't even think about touching me."

"Ya know ya want it, bitch." He grabs his crotch, tugs at himself suggestively. Reaches out, tries to grab her left shoulder.

She backs out of his reach. "Don't touch me."

"Touch you any time I want." He reaches for her shoulder a second time.

She pulls a riding crop out of one of the shopping bags. Whips him across the left side of his face, two good swipes.

"You cocksucker." He reaches out again. Grabs her right wrist, the one holding the riding crop. Twists her wrist behind her back, judo style. Keeps twisting until she drops the whip.

"You bastard." She slaps his face with her left hand.

"You're askin' for it, bitch." He makes a fist with his right hand. Cocks it to throw a punch. "I oughta punch your fuckin' lights out."

"Go ahead, dodo, and wind up back in jail before I hit the floor."

He holds the pose. Wants to retaliate. But eventually unclenches his fist and lowers his hand.

"You ain't worth goin' to jail for," he says. "But trust me, bitch, you'll be sorry."

—

My Uber app pings.

"Hang on," I tell My Friend. "Just got a ride."

"Where?"

I look at the app:

Sam
2800 Columbus Boulevard
Philadelphia

"Looks like a topless club."

"Maybe you'll get lucky," he says.

"Doubt it. Some guy named Sam. Besides, I don't talk to the strippers."

"Why not?" he asks.

"Don't want anything misconstrued. Don't need any complaints about their driver coming on to them."

"You worry too much," he says.

"Maybe. Almost there. Talk to ya tomorrow."

—

I see a bright purple neon sign: **BABES IN TOYLAND.**

Pull over and call the rider. Two rings before a man's voice answers, "Hello."

"Your ride's here. Silver SUV with the flashers blinking. Right out front."

"Oh," he says, "the, uh, ride's for one of my girls. Pull right up to the, uh, entrance. I'll tell her you're here."

—

Back inside the strip club.

The manager's short and stocky. Name's Sam. Looks 40, but just turned 31. Walks up to the bouncer. "Did you, uh, see Jade?"

"Just seen her." Points toward the coatroom.

"What, uh, happened to your face?"

"Nuthin."

"Looks like something happened."

"She accidentally hit me with her fuckin' whip, "the bouncer says. "You know, just fuckin' around."

"Looks like a handprint on the other side."

"Like I said," the bouncer says. "Just fuckin' around."

"Please," the manager says, "no horsing around." He spots the stripper exiting the coatroom. "Jade."

She's carrying her makeup case and the two shopping bags. Smiles at the manager, gives the bouncer a dirty look.

"Your, uh, Uber's here," the manager says. "Silver SUV with its, uh, lights blinking. Driver's name is Steve."

—

I see a tall brunette exit the strip club and start approaching my vehicle. She's holding a makeup case in her left hand, struggling to carry two shopping bags with her right.

I exit the driver's door. Head around to the back of the vehicle. Get there at the same time she does.

"You Steve?" she asks.

"Yep."

"I'm Jade."

"Pleased to meet you, Jade."

I open the hatch. Start packing her belongings. First comes the makeup case, heavier than it looks. Next comes one of the shopping bags. Something falls out and lands on the ground. Looks like a riding crop. Guess it's one of her props.

She bends down, picks it up with her left hand. Stands back up, hands it to me. "Just stick it in one of the bags."

I stick it in the second bag.

She's already opening the back door on the passenger's side. Getting inside the vehicle.

I close the hatch, return back behind the wheel.

"All set?" I ask.

"All set."

I hit **START TRIP** on the app, see her destination:

340 Media Station Road
Media

I know exactly where that is. But I'm not sure about the shortest route between the strip club and the entrance to I-95.

Start pulling away. The GPS tells me to make a right turn, but I'm looking at a **DO NOT ENTER** sign. I stop.

"Go ahead," she says. "If you get stopped, I can fix it. I know all the cops around here. Plus I gotta lotta pull at City Hall."

"No kidding."

"Yeah," she says. "Ever since I started blowing one of the judges."

I'm both stunned and intrigued by her candor. Wanta hear more. "No kidding?"

"My old boyfriend got arrested last year," she says. "Charged with criminal assault. I asked one of my cop buddies and found out who the judge was. Arranged a meeting, and that's when I started blowing him."

The strategy worked to perfection. She not only succeeded in getting her boyfriend's charges reduced to a misdemeanor, but eventually got the case dismissed.

So I drive down the street the wrong way.

She talks nonstop for the next 20 minutes. All the way to her apartment complex.

"I only moved here a couple months ago," she says.

"How do you like it so far?"

"So far," she says, "so good. But my next-door neighbor's a nosey bitch. She's got, like, a camera outside her apartment. And she's always sticking her nose in my business."

"No kidding."

She laughs. "I ran into her in the hall yesterday. She tells me she knows my boyfriend's 5-11. Then she says she saw me come home with a guy who's 6-4."

"No kidding."

"Yeah," she says. "So I tell her, 'Since you're so into my shit, why don't you come over and trim my pussy hair next time it needs trimming.'"

We're both laughing as I pull into the complex.

"What building?"

"A."

I drive up a steep hill. Pass two buildings on the way up.

"Which entrance?"

"All the way at the end," she says.

Turn right, drive 100 yards to reach the last entrance.

"How's this?"

"Perfect," she says. "Oh, I forgot to thank you for loading my things into your car when we left the club."

"No problem."

"I don't usually have this much to carry," she says, "but someone gave me a bunch of presents today."

"Birthday?"

"No," she says. "He's, like, a secret admirer."

"You ever see Fatal Attraction?"

"What's that?"

"A movie."

"What's it about?" she asks.

"A secret admirer, and boiling a rabbit in a pot."

"Doesn't sound like Alice in Wonderland," she says.

"Trust me, it's not. How well do you know your secret admirer?"

"Let's just say–" she starts to explain, then stops abruptly.

"Sorry. Didn't mean to pry."

"Not that," she says. "It's, well, my wrist is starting to hurt like a sonavabitch."

"How'd you hurt it?"

"An argument before you picked me up. An old boyfriend. The one I already told you about. The one I got outta trouble last year."

"On the assault charge?"

"Yeah." She leans forward. "One of the bouncers. Sal. But he won't accept the fact I broke up with him. He's still, like, possessive. Thinks he owns me."

"Sorry to hear that." I turn my head, see her face for the first time. Quite pretty.

"We had a good thing going," she says. "But then the asshole started screwing around on me. Didn't know for sure at first. But then he started acting funny. So I asked him about it."

"And he confessed?"

"No way," she says. "Asshole lied to my face."

"Then how do you know for sure?"

"Caught the motherfucker in the act," she says.

"No kidding."

"Yeah," she says. "Caught him screwing one of the other girls. A bimbo who calls herself Charity. Trust me, she gives it up just like her name says."

We laugh.

"And you'll never guess where I caught them."

"No clue."

"In a fucking utility closet," she says.

"Sounds like *prima facie* evidence to me."

"Not sure what that means," she says. "That *prima–*"

"*Prima facie*. It's Latin for 'essential.' Means 'at first look' or 'on its face.' It's the type of evidence accepted in court as being true, unless, or until, someone can prove otherwise."

"You used to be a lawyer or something?" she asks.

"Not really. Just know about things like that."

"Anyway," she says, "tonight the asshole says he wants to drive me home."

"What's wrong with that?"

"He didn't wanta drive me home. Just wanted to get me outside, into his car, so I could suck his cock. But when I said no, he tried to bully me."

"No kidding."

She leans closer. "He got a little grabby, so I whacked him across the face with my whip."

"The one–"

"Right," she says. "That one. Got him good. Twice. And that really pissed him off. So the fucker grabbed my wrist and twisted it behind my back."

"Might be sprained."

"Starting to swell a little." She wiggles her wrist, probes it gently. "Here, feel it." She extends her right hand over the front seat.

I take her hand, gently touch the wrist area.

"Ouch." She jerks her hand back reflexively.

"It does feel swollen."

"And it hurts," she says. "Would you be willing to help me once again?"

CHAPTER 2

"He's being a dick," a female says.

Her name's Jessika but she goes by Jess. She's sitting on a sectional sofa in the living room of her condominium. Talking to her best friend on her cellphone. Dressed comfortably in a robe and slippers. Holding a glass of wine, half full, in her free hand.

"Does he know you got fired?" her best friend asks. Her name's Margo.

"Texted him. Said I needed to talk to him. But he never got back to me. So I called, left the same message on his voicemail. Said it was important, but he still didn't call. So I texted: 'I just got fired please call me.'"

"And he still didn't call?" Margo asks.

"No." Jess swallows what's left in the wine glass. "Texted twice more, called twice more, but the dick never got back to me."

"Maybe something came up at work," Margo says.

"How long does it take to text? Just wanted a shoulder to cry on. But the dick refused to be there when I needed him most."

"Think he's cheating on you?" Margo asks.

"Not until you just mentioned it."

"Notice any signs?" Margo asks.

"Like what?"

"Lipstick on his collar?" Margo asks.

"No. Never saw anything suspicious."

"You know how I caught Roger," Margo says. "Right?"

"Told me a million times. Cum stains on his shorts."

"Ever check Pablo's shorts?" Margo asks.

"I don't go snooping through his clothes."

"Maybe it's time you started," Margo says. "Just saying. So what're you going to do now?"

"About what?"

"Pablo," Margo says.

"First I need to find a new job. Fast. Mortgage to pay, bills to pay, and still a few years left on my student loan."

"One hanging over my head, too," Margo says.

"How long did it take you to get over Roger?"

"Less than a minute," Margo says. "Maybe Pablo's got some bitch on the side."

"You think he'd do something like?"

"They all do," Margo says. "For all you know, you might be *his* bitch on the side."

Jess sets the wine glass on an end table. Gets up, starts walking down the hallway. "Maybe it's my fault. Maybe he doesn't find me attractive anymore. You think I'm losing it?"

"Crazy talk," Margo says. "You're gorgeous."

Jess flips on the light switch as she enters the bathroom. Takes a good look at her reflection in the mirror. Tweaks her hair, smiles. "Guess you're right."

"Exactly," Margo says.

Jess enters the kitchen. Stops in front of the refrigerator. Opens the door, removes a bottle of Yellow Tail Merlot. "Anyone new in your life?"

"I wish," Margo says. "But five months without a nibble."

"Sorry you broke it off?"

"Only when I crawl into bed," Margo says, "and no one's crawling on top of me. To tell you the truth, I could use a good lay."

"What're you doing right now?"

"Getting ready for bed," Margo says. "Why?"

"Can I talk you into going out for a drink?"

"Almost midnight," Margo says. "Already dressed for bed and have to get up early in the morning. We'll get together tomorrow."

CHAPTER 3

I'm still behind the Media Station Apartments, staring at a 6-foot chain-link fence. Steep drop-off on the other side. Trash dumpster on the right.

I back up slowly. Pull forward slowly. Only way to avoid bumping any cars parked on both sides of me. Two more backups before I finally turn all the way around. But here comes a car with its high beams blinding me.

Come on, pal, gimme a fuckin' break. Barely enough room to squeeze past each other. But this sonavabitch isn't slowing down.

Should I stop and let the asshole pass? Or take my chances and keep going?

Fuck him. Damn the torpedoes. Full speed ahead.

We almost sideswipe but pass without colliding. Car looks like a Beamer. Too dark to see the driver's face, but definitely a man behind the wheel.

I turn on the Uber app and get a request:

Jessika
1030 East Lancaster Avenue
Bryn Mawr

The app sets the parameters at 13 miles and 19 minutes to reach the pickup location.

Retrace my route back through Media. Get on the Blue Route, head northbound. Not much traffic. Only takes 15 minutes to reach my exit. Another 4 minutes to reach the pickup location.

A condo complex called the Radnor House sits off to the right. Ten stories tall, but looks taller because it's perched on top of a hill.

I start up a crescent-shaped driveway. Halfway up the hill I call the rider.

A female's voice answers, "Hello."

"This is your Uber driver. I'm right outside the entrance in a silver SUV."

"Thanks. Getting on the elevator right now."

Two minutes pass.

The sliding doors open automatically and a female exits the building. Looks attractive. A little better than average height, blondish hair. Trim and athletic-looking. Wearing tight jeans and a navy sweater.

She starts walking toward the passenger side. When she gets close, I lower the window on her side.

She looks through the open window. "Steve?"

"Yep."

She opens the back door, gets inside.

"Where we going?" I ask while closing the window.

"Phoenixville. Know where it is?"

"Yep. You live there?"

"No," she says. "I live here."

"Don't mind me for being curious. But if you live here, why are you going to Phoenixville at this hour?"

"Just decided to spend the night at my parents' place."

"Why?"

"Guess you could say I had a fight with my boyfriend. And in case you haven't noticed, I've been drinking."

"Doesn't show."

"Believe me," she says. "Been drinking wine all day and I can really feel it now. No way I'm driving. Last thing I need is a DUI on top of everything else."

"Smart move."

I hit **START TRIP** and see her destination:

909 Westridge Drive
Phoenixville

The app says 30 minutes and 16 miles. Do some quick factoring. It'll be around 2 a.m. by the time I drop her off. Decide this is my last ride.

Put the car in gear and we're on our way.

"I'm not usually like this," she says. "But I got fired today."

"I got fired once. Not a whole lotta fun. Plus you think you're never gonna find another job."

"Starting to feel like that already," she says.

"What kinda work you do?"

"Bartender at the Paramour," she says. "At least I was until today."

"Interesting name. Once bought a gym membership for my girlfriend and wrote 'paramour' to describe our relationship. But no one knew what it meant."

"I don't either," she says.

"Literally, it means 'for love.' Usually implies an illicit partner to a married man. Pretty much the same as mistress."

"Oh."

"But I used it wrong."

"How's that?" she asks.

"Neither one of us were married. Ergo, nothing illicit going on. Shoulda just said girlfriend, but I was trying to show off."

"Thanks for the vocabulary lesson," she says.

"Welcome. But why'd you get fired?"

"New owner," she says. "Brought in a new manager. The new manager wanted to hire his girlfriend. Made up some bullshit excuse and I was out."

"How long you work there?"

"Going on five years," she says. "Great job. Made enough to afford the condo where you picked me up."

"Impressive. Main Line address. Not cheap."

"Tell me about it," she says. "But I never planned on being a bartender in the first place."

"What'd you wanta be?"

"Graduated from the Art Institute in Philly," she says. "But didn't take long to figure out being an artist wasn't in the cards."

"Why not?"

"Not good enough," she says. "But, trust me, I make a lot more tending bar than I ever would painting pictures. So, let's face it, I'm a bartender."

"Nothing wrong with that. How'd you get into art to begin with?"

"My art teacher pushed me," she says. "I could draw a little, and being an artist sounded romantic."

"I know where you're coming from. I wanta be a mystery writer. That sounds romantic to a lotta people, but I haven't sold a single story so far. So that's where romance ends and reality begins. So, for now, I'm a glorified taxi driver."

"How's that working out for you?" she asks.

"Pays the bills. Set my own hours. Plenty of flexibility. Plenty of time to write."

"I see," she says. "And how do things stand with your girlfriend?"

"What girlfriend?"

"Your paramour."

"Oh." I chuckle. "Old news. No girlfriend."

"Not even one?" she asks.

"Nope."

"Why not?" she asks.

"Ambition."

"Ambition?" She sounds puzzled. "I don't get it."

"Ambition is my tragic flaw of character."

"Since when is ambition a flaw?" she asks.

"Not usually. But in my case it is."

"How so?" she asks.

"Like I said. Wanta be a mystery writer. So bad. But my stories keep getting rejected."

"Why?"

"No idea. I think they're pretty good."

"Still," she says, "you keep trying."

"Yep. Getting a story published is just my initial goal. Then comes a book, then more books. Then seeing one of my books turned into a movie. Or a Netflix series."

"You do have some pretty lofty goals," she says. "But maybe ambition isn't your tragic flaw after all."

"No? What is?"

"Maybe ego's your tragic flaw," she says.

"How so?"

"Hate to say it," she says, "But maybe, just like me being an artist, you're just not good enough to be a writer."

"Hmmm. Never looked at it that way. Hope you're wrong. But either way, ambition or ego, I'm determined to make it."

"Where do you stand now?" she asks.

"Submitted another story last week. Waiting to hear back."

"What do you do for fun?" she asks.

"Not much."

"All work and no play make Jack a dull boy."

"Just call me Jack. But enough about me. You still didn't tell me about the fight with your boyfriend."

"Oh that," she says. "Getting fired was a real downer. Never saw it coming. Tried to contact him, looking for some sympathy. Called, texted, but the dick ignored me."

"How long you been going out with this guy?"

"Met him in art school," she says. "Bumped into each other at a party last year, and one thing led to another."

"What's he do?"

"Owns his own business," she says. "A start-up. Can I ask you a question."

"Shoot."

"And get an honest answer?"

"Shoot."

"If you were in his shoes," she says, "would you call me? Or at least text me?"

"No way you're getting me in the middle of this."

"Seriously," she says. "What would you do?"

"Um, honestly. If you were someone I cared about, really cared about, I'd get back to you ASAP."

"There's a Wawa up ahead," she says. "Would you be so kind to stop? I need to put something in my stomach, you know, a doughnut or something, to soak up the alcohol."

I pull into the Wawa parking lot, find a spot in front.

She gets out. Comes around, stops alongside my window.

I lower the window.

"You want something?" she asks.

"No, I'm fine. Thanks anyway."

"My treat," she says.

"Really. I'm fine."

"I want to get you something," she insists.

"Okay, you win. I'll take a blueberry doughnut."

"No way they have any blueberry doughnuts," she says. "Seriously, what do you want?"

"Trust me. Against my principles to lie. They have blueberry doughnuts."

"Don't worry," she says. "I'll surprise you."

She walks away and enters the Wawa.

—

Three or four minutes pass.

She's carrying a small paper bag when she exits. Comes right over to my window.

I lower the window.

"They did have blueberry doughnuts," she says.

"Told you so."

"Would you mind if I sit up in front?" she asks.

"Not at all."

She walks around. Opens the door, gets in. "Couldn't believe they had blueberry doughnuts. Got one for myself, too. Look, are you in a hurry?"

"Not really. Gonna quit after I drop you off. Why?"

"Go through Valley Forge Park," she says. "Takes a little longer, but it's a nicer ride."

I set course for Valley Forge Park.

The doughnuts are long gone by the time we reach a narrow road leading into the park. Passed a handful of cars on the way here, but now we're the only vehicle on the road. Without any other headlights, the ride's dark. We're talking openly. Getting to know each other little by little. Under different circumstances some might call it romantic.

Suddenly she touches my right bicep gently. I glance at her hand momentarily, then look back at the road.

Now both hands are caressing my right bicep. "Do you mind if I touch you like this?" she asks.

"Does it make you feel better?"

"In my current state of affairs," she says, "and my current state of alcohol consumption." She giggles. "Yes. Yes, it does."

"Then I don't mind at all."

"Call me crazy," she says, "but I just came up with a slight change of plan."

"Like what?"

"I'd like to buy you a drink," she says.

"No problem. When do you wanta get together?"

"You don't understand," she says. "*Right now*. I want to buy you a drink *right now*."

"It's almost one o'clock and we're in the middle of nowhere."

"This is where I grew up," she says. "I know a place where we can get a drink. Still open and not far from here."

—

It takes six minutes to reach a one-story building standing by itself on a small lot. The sign's still lit: **BLACK HORSE TAVERN.**

Looks pretty much like your corner bar, but this corner bar's in the middle of nowhere. Three cars parked in the lot. Spaced far apart. Makes it easy to pull into a spot near the entrance.

Next thing I know we're holding hands as we enter.

Casual inside. A long U-shaped bar. Several big-screen TVs on the walls. Pool table at the other end of the room. Two guys shooting pool.

"I have to go to the lady's room," She releases my hand. "But you don't have to wait for me to order." She keeps walking toward the far end of the building.

No one's at the bar, so I sit on the stool closest to me.

The bartender comes right over. "What can I get for you?"

"Bottle of Bud. But I wanta wait until she gets back."

"No problem." He walks away.

I sit there watching the two guys shooting pool.

Jess returns a little while later. Kisses me on the cheek. Sits on the stool next to me.

The bartender returns.

"What can I get for you folks?" he asks.

Jess turns her head toward me.

"Bottle of Bud," I tell the bartender. "No glass."

"And you?" the bartender asks Jess.

"I've seen you before," Jess tells the bartender, "but don't know your name."

"Jimmy."

"I'm Jess."

"Pleased to meet you, Jess," the bartender says. "What can I get for you?"

"Same as Steve," she says, "but I'll take a glass."

The bartender nods, starts walking away.

"Jimmy," she calls out.

The bartender stops, turns back to face her.

"And I'll take a shot of Cuervo." She turns to face me. "Want a shot?"

"No. I'm good."

"My treat," she says.

"Thanks, but I still hafta drive home."

The bartender starts to walk away again.

"Jimmy," she calls out again.

He stops walking, turns back to face her.

"Make that a double."

CHAPTER 4

It's a little before 4:30 by the time I get home, still dark. Tired as hell, but something needs addressing before I can even think about going to sleep.

Open the door. Take ten steps into the living room.

Rectangular in shape. More like an office than a living room. A gray sofa sits next to the wall on the right. Picked it out because it's 90 inches long, allows me to stretch my legs to take a nap without folding them.

A coffee table sits in front of the sofa. But the sofa and coffee table are the only pieces of living-room furniture in the living room. Unless you count the big-screen TV on the opposite wall.

A wide desk butts up against the wall to the left of the TV. A three-drawer file cabinet sits to the right of the desk. A tall bookcase sits to the left of the desk.

One look at the bookcase leaves little doubt about my focus: In Cold Blood, The Godfather, The Carpetbaggers, Helter Skelter, Born to Be Wild, Silence of the Lambs, Compulsion, God's Pocket, Mitigating Circumstances, Rosemary's Baby, Cape Fear, Nightmares in Pink, The Black Dahlia, Mr. Majestyk, Glitz, One Flew Over the Cuckoo's Nest, The Adventurers, The Dreadful Lemon Sky, and The Valachi Papers.

A black leather executive chair, one that leans back and swivels, sits in front of the desk.

I settle into the executive chair. A laptop sits on the desktop. A printer's off to the left.

I open the laptop. A couple clicks take me to my inbox. One from OneDrive about photos I uploaded yesterday. Like I didn't already know that. One from Uber trying to lure me into leasing a vehicle from them. Rip off. Not interested. And here's one from the Ellery Queen Mystery Magazine.

That's what I'm looking for. Cross my fingers. Open it and take a look.

"Motherfucker!"

It says: **Dear Writer–Doesn't Meet Our Standards.**

Another rejection slip. Short, not sweet. That's three from Ellery Queen to go along with three from Alfred Hitchcock.

This story's called "A Taste for Revenge."

More than anything else, I wanta get my first story published. But it's getting to the point where I suspect the editors see my name and categorize me as a hack. Then they toss my story onto the slush pile without reading it and send me the robotic rejection slip.

Maybe that Jess was right. Maybe it's time to face the fact I'm just not good enough. If I can't sell a stinking 5,000-word story to a mystery magazine, how in the world am I gonna get a book published?

They attached my story to the email. I click the attachment to open the file. Takes 15 minutes to read the story from end to end. As objectively as possible.

But, damn, like I just said, this *is* a good story. One that could be, and should be, published. A market exists somewhere. I just hafta find it.

CHAPTER 5

Happy Hour that afternoon.

Jess is sitting at the bar when her cellphone rings. "Hello."

"You there already?" Margo's voice on the phone.

"Middle of the bar. Saved you a seat."

They're meeting at The Grog Grill on Lancaster Avenue in the heart of Bryn Mawr. A chic Irish tavern like you might find in Dublin.

Jess is finishing her drink when Margo arrives.

Margo's good-looking. A sleek blonde who exudes confidence. No hugs or handshakes when she reaches Jess. Friends since kindergarten, they see each other often.

"Just in time." Jess sets her empty glass on the bar.

The bartender arrives just as Margo sits next to Jess.

"Hey, Margo," he says. "What can I get for you?"

Margo looks at Jess's glass. "What's that?"

"What's left of a martini," Jess says.

"Pass," Margo says. "I'll take a Manhattan. No, wait. Make it a Margarita."

"Frozen?" the bartender asks.

"Talked me into it." Margo smiles.

"Another martini for me," Jess says.

"Aye-aye." The bartender walks away.

"Any luck today?" Margo asks.

"Didn't get a chance to go job-hunting, if that's what you mean. But got lucky last night. In fact, real lucky."

"You and Pablo made up?" Margo asks.

"No way."

"Went to stay with my parents last night. Took an Uber, and the driver was gorgeous. So we went to the Black Horse and had a couple drinks."

"And?"

"And we did it."

"Get the fuck outta here," Margo asks.

"Seriously. We did."

"Where?" Margo asks.

"In the parking lot."

"Let's see if I got this right," Margo says. "You screwed an Uber driver? In the parking lot? Outside the Black Horse?"

"Right, right, and right."

"I don't believe it," Margo says.

"Believe it." Jess is smiling, almost ready to giggle.

"Sounds like a spite-fuck to me," Margo says.

"Maybe that's how it started."

"And how did it end?" Margo asks.

"Maybe it didn't end. Maybe I want someone who's there when I need him."

"And you think this Uber driver," Margo says, "this stranger you met less than 24 hours ago, you think he'll be there when you need him."

"Steve. His name's Steve. He listened to my problems, Margo. About getting fired. About Pablo ignoring me. I mean, he *really* listened."

"He saw you were drunk," Margo says, "knew you were vulnerable, and scored an easy piece of ass."

"Wasn't like that at all. He was sympathetic and empathetic. If anything, I talked him into doing it."

"Sure you did," Margo says.

"Seriously, I was the aggressor. Anyway, I got his number."

The bartender returns with the drinks.

"Thank you." Margo nods.

"Put them on my tab," Jess says.

"Aye-aye." The bartender moves away to take care of a couple at the end of the bar.

"So now what?" Margo asks.

"I want to explore my options."

"And how exactly do you plan to do that?"

"Juggle them."

Margo laughs out loud. "You can't handle Pablo by himself. How the hell you going to juggle both of them?"

"I think I can do it."

"For crying out loud," Margo says. "You're actually thinking about pitting Pablo up against this stranger? This Uber driver?"

"He's not just an Uber driver."

"No," Margo challenges. "Who is he? The Prince of fucking Denmark?"

"Ha-ha. Very funny, Shakespeare. But since you asked, he wants to be a mystery writer. And his ultimate goal is to turn his books into a movie. Or a TV series."

"Then why isn't he living in L.A.?" Margo asks.

"Didn't ask him that. But, please, give him a chance. Wait till you meet him."

"How, when, and where is that going to happen?"

"Don't know yet." Jess sips her martini, slips into thought.

Several moments pass.

Jess slams the glass on the bar, snaps her fingers.

—

I'm stretched out on the couch in my underwear, watching an episode of Better Call Saul when my cellphone rings.

I grab the phone off the coffee table. Look at the caller ID, get a surprise. "Hello."

"Steve," a female's voice says. "This is Jess, from last night. Remember me?"

"How could I forget?"

"This is short notice," she says, "but I just got an idea."

"I'm listening."

"Love to get together with you again," she says. "So I have a proposition for you."

"You have my attention."

"How soon can you get here?" she asks.

—

Warrant's "Cherry Pie" is blasting out of 5,000-watt speakers and floodlights are casting an indigo hue over the entire room. And thanks to businessmen flocking in for Happy Hour, the room's close to capacity.

A blonde's working the pole. Tall and leggy. Calls herself Candi.

Strobe lights are pulsating in time with the music. Each ray pinpoints the sequin on her gold lamé G-string and sends reflections shooting back toward the audience. Other than that G-string, already stuffed with cash, she's down to a cowboy hat and boots.

Candi moves to the edge of the runway. Winks at a man sitting at the bar right in front of her. He's been eyeballing her all through her routine. She smiles. Pulls down the front of her G-string to give him a peek.

He reaches into a pocket without moving his eyes. Pulls out some cash.

She moves closer.

He inserts a $10 into her G-string.

She blows him a kiss, starts retreating.

"Cherry Pie" fades and "American Woman" starts playing. The Lenny Kravitz version. The volume's low enough to allow the emcee's voice to come booming out of the P.A. system.

"Hey, hey, ladies and gentlemen. Let's hear it for Candi." Pauses for enthusiastic applause as Candi exits the stage. "And now, let's bring out our next beautiful showgirl ... with a great big Babes in Toyland welcome. Clap your hands for Jade."

"American Woman" starts blasting.

Jade should be entering the stage, but she's not.

Five seconds pass. The music keeps pounding, but Jade's still nowhere in sight.

"Where's Jade?" a female's voice asks. The voice has a twinge of a French accent. She's wearing a harem outfit and has that Middle-Eastern look – dark hair, dark eyes, and darkish skin. She's standing in the back of the room next to a bouncer.

"I don't see her," the bouncer says.

"No shit, Sherlock."

—

Still topless, Candi enters the dressing room pulling bill after bill out of her G-string.

The room's rectangular and small, but efficient. Mirrors on the walls. Dressing stations every five feet. Counters filled with makeup, hair dryers, and curling irons.

A pink-haired dancer is standing in front of a mirror, primping and preening. Two more dancers are sitting at dressing stations doing the same thing. And two more are standing in the middle of the room.

All wearing skimpy bras and thong bikinis.

One dancer takes off her top. The dancer standing next to her sprays coconut oil all over her back, starts spreading the oil evenly.

The dancer in the harem outfit enters the room. "Where's Jade?"

"Ain't seen her," says the girl spreading the oil.

"Next girl up."

—

The manager's sitting behind his desk when someone knocks on the door. "Come in."

The door opens, the harem girl enters. She calls herself Farrah. She's 25, born in Morocco, moved to Philly during her teens. "Jade's not here," she informs him.

"That's not, uh, like her," the manager says. "Is it?"

"Jade's never late."

"You, uh, text her," he says. "I'll give her a call."

The manager picks up his cellphone. Calls, but gets no answer. Waits for the call to go to voicemail. "Jade, this is Sam from the, uh, club. Just wondering where you are. Please give us a call."

He looks across the desk at the harem girl.

"I just texted her," she says. "No reply."

—

The Grog's crowded, but I can Jess sitting at the bar.

She sees me. Lifts up off her stool, waves.

Looks like she's with someone else. I'm good at profiling. Their body language tells me they're best friends.

I reach Jess.

She kisses me on the cheek. "This is my best friend Margo."

"And you're Steve," Margo says with a warm smile.

"Yep." I return her smile. She seems friendly.

"Barkeep," Jess calls out. When the bartender looks in her direction, she waves him over. "Can we get–" She looks at me.

"Bottle of Bud. Save the glass."

"And back us up," Jess says.

I remain standing in between them.

"No sense beating around the bush," Jess says. "Do you have any plans for tomorrow night?"

"Nothing I can think of. Why? What's up?"

"I'm throwing a party," she says, "and I'm inviting you."

Her invitation puzzles me. "Thought you have a boyfriend."

"She does," Margo says.

"Then how–?" I start to ask Jess.

"Simple," Jess says. "You pretend to be Margo's new boyfriend."

I look at Margo. "You all right with that?"

"I don't have a crystal ball," Margo says, "but this is one of the dumbest ideas I ever heard."

"Then why–?" I start to ask.

"Relax," Margo interrupts. "Jess told me all about you two, hence my skepticism. But she's determined to carry out her crazy plan."

"I don't think it's so crazy," Jess says.

"I do," Margo says. "But under duress, I agree to go along with the charade."

"But what–?" I start to ask again.

"Don't worry," Margo says. "I'm good at playing along."

—

The sun's starting to set as a late-model red Camaro moves down the driveway behind Jade's apartment building. Farrah's behind the wheel. Candi's riding shotgun.

"Last entrance," Candi instructs her.

Farrah drives to the end of the driveway. Parks. Kills the engine.

Both front doors swing open, both girls exit the vehicle, now wearing sweaters, tight jeans, and boots.

Candi leads the way toward the building. Farrah keeps pace a step behind. They climb nine steps to reach the stoop outside the entrance. A panel of buttons is inset into the wall, a little below eye-level.

"Step one," Candi says, "is ring the right bell."

She stoops down to get a good look at the panel. Runs her index finger along the buttons. Finds the one for Apartment 201, presses it.

They wait several seconds but get no response.

"Step two." Candi presses the button again.

Several more seconds pass without a response.

Candi starts to press the button a third time, but Farrah pushes her hand aside.

"Step three." Farrah presses all the buttons.

Five seconds later come a couple buzzes.

Farrah opens the door, they enter. Inside are two stairways. The one on the right goes up, the one on left goes down.

"Which way?" Farrah asks.

"Up one flight."

Farrah leads the way. Reaches the first landing. Opens the fire door, enters a large vestibule. "Which way?"

"To the right," Candi says. "Apartment 201."

Farrah knocks on the door in a rapid staccato.

They wait a few seconds but get no response.

Candi pounds on the door with both fists.

Unbeknownst to them, the door adjacent to Apartment 201 opens a pinch.

They continue knocking and pounding for another minute, but never get a response.

—

Candi and Farrah exit the building. Start walking briskly toward the red Camaro.

"Now what?" Farrah asks.

"Let's call a locksmith."

"Can we do that?" Farrah wonders.

"Duh?"

"I know we *can* do that," Farrah says. "But will a locksmith open the door on our say-so alone? Or should we call the cops?"

Ask and ye shall be answered.

A siren's blaring and emergency lights are flashing as a police car comes speeding down the driveway toward them. Stops behind the Camaro.

A uniformed officer exits the car.

"There they are," a woman in her 60s yells at the officer. She's standing on the stoop outside the entrance to the building. Points at Farrah and Candi. "Right there by that red car."

A backup police car arrives.

A uniformed officer exits that car. Starts looking around, trying to analyze the situation.

Both officers come face to face with Farrah and Candi.

The old woman walks right up to the four of them.

"These two don't live here," she tells the officers. "But they were just causing an awful disturbance outside my door with all their knocking and pounding."

"Is that true?" the lead officer asks.

"Our friend didn't show up for work," Farrah tells the officer. "We called her, and texted, but never got a response. We were worried. So our boss sent us to check on her. We knocked on her door but didn't get an answer."

The officer turns toward the woman. "Where's the manager's office?"

—

The complex manager uses a master key to unlock the door to Apartment 201. In his early 30s, he wears his hair in a man bun, sports a scruffy beard, and wears tight jeans.

He unlocks the door. Opens it, steps aside.

Both officers enter the apartment cautiously.

The manager stops just inside the door.

Nothing looks out of place or disturbed. Still, the officers unfasten the straps on their duty holsters, draw their weapons.

"What's her name?" the lead officer asks.

"Forsythe," the manager says. "Rita Forsythe."

"Rita," the officer calls out. "Miss Forsythe."

The officers gesture to each other to indicate splitting up. The lead officer heads down a hallway leading further inside. The backup officer takes the living room.

The manager holds his ground in the vestibule.

Several seconds pass.

"Down here," the lead officer calls out. He's standing halfway down the long hallway.

The backup officer reaches him within seconds.

The manager, yielding to curiosity, follows behind.

All three men are now standing outside the bathroom door, looking inside.

"Holy shit," the manager says.

CHAPTER 6

Two backup officers start sealing the apartment with yellow crime-scene tape.

The lead officer contacts the county's Criminal Investigation Division. "We found a white female," he tells the dispatcher, "dead at the Media Station Apartments. Inside Apartment 201. Looks like a drug overdose."

The dispatcher relays the message to the Medical Examiner, to Operations, and to Forensics. A medical examiner, two detectives, and two evidence technicians are soon enroute to the complex.

—

A man carrying a medical valise arrives first. Dr. Kenneth Nakamura, 53, the county medical examiner.

He climbs the interior stairway at a brisk pace. Soon reaches the landing on the second floor. Opens the fire door, sees yellow tape crisscrossing the open doorway of Apartment 201.

Two uniformed officers are standing on the other side of the tape. The lead officer sees him coming.

"No need to rush, doc," the officer says. "She's dead."

"Then I guess I am not needed here," Dr. Nakamura jokes.

"Good one, doc." The officer separates the strands of tape to make it easier for him to enter.

Dr. Nakamura ducks under the tape. "Where is the individual in question?"

"I called it in as accidental OD," the officer says.

"I will keep that in mind," Dr. Nakamura says. "But things are not always as they seem. Which way, please?"

"This way, doc." The officer leads him down the hallway. Stops outside the bathroom door, steps aside.

Dr. Nakamura stops at the marble threshold, looks inside the bathroom. Sets his valise on the floor. Opens it, takes out a camera.

Careful not to disturb anything, he steps inside. Approaches the bathtub. Stops. Starts snapping. Takes nine pictures. Places the camera back inside the valise, removes a recorder.

"Victim appears to be a white female," he begins. "Body in prone position inside bathtub. Appears to be nude. Head somewhat elevated above surface of bathwater. Body submerged beneath bathwater. Quantity of bubbles floating on surface. Obscuring bulk of body beneath surface. Approximate age appears to be within two years of 24."

Takes a pair of rubber gloves out of his valise. Puts them on, steps toward the body. Presses his fingers against the victim's carotid artery. Holds that position for several seconds.

"Victim dead at scene. Time of death appears to be 12 to 18 hours prior to discovery of body."

Sticks a thermometer in the water. "Observe dangling earrings, gold, both ears. Also observe heart-shaped necklace, gold, around victim's neck." Removes the thermometer from the water, looks at it. "Water temperature: 68 degrees."

Looks around the room. His eyes stop at the vanity next to the sink.

"Observe small mirror on vanity next to sink. Said mirror rectangular in shape. Approximately 4 inches by 6 inches. Observe powdery white residue on surface of mirror. Also observe one razor blade, single edge, next to said mirror."

He retrieves the camera, snaps pictures of the vanity. Steps closer to get a better look.

"Observe one small plastic baggie next to said mirror. Approximately 2 inches by 3 inches. Also observe similar white powdery residue inside baggie."

Pauses the recorder.

"Like I said, doc," the officer says, "accidental OD."

"When you find drug paraphernalia in close proximity to the victim," Dr. Nakamura replies, "for sure, 99 times out of 100, you are looking at a drug overdose. So your impulse is probably correct. But what do you make of the fact that this poor soul is still wearing her jewelry?"

"To tell the truth, doc," the officer responds, "I can't see any jewelry from where I'm standing."

"I see."

Dr. Nakamura goes back to his valise, removes a pair of tweezers. Uses the tweezers to lift the baggie, carefully, high enough to get a good look at the reverse side of the baggie.

—

Detectives Pam Bishop and Donald Chase arrive at the scene. Appear to be in their early 30s.

Det. Bishop is a brunette, shapely, moderately attractive.

Det. Chase is tall and thin, sporting a few days of uneven stubble.

The backup officer escorts them down the hall to the bathroom. There, they encounter Dr. Nakamura, who's still assessing the scene.

"Notice anything, Pam?" Dr. Nakamura asks.

"Other than the drug paraphernalia on the vanity?"

"We will get back to that momentarily." Dr. Nakamura smiles. "Yes. But other than that, do you notice anything out of the ordinary?"

Exercising caution, she steps inside the bathroom. Looks at the body in the bathtub. "She's still wearing her earrings and necklace."

"Very observant," Dr. Nakamura says. "Now, as the only female present, when you take a bath, assuming you take baths and not showers, do you wear your jewelry? Or do you remove it?"

"Makes no difference," she says. "Everything comes off. Unless I'm in a hurry. Then I might leave my earrings in, but not dangling ones like that."

"As I thought." Dr. Nakamura steps toward the vanity. "Now take a look at this and tell me what you think."

He uses the tweezers to lift the baggie. Flips the baggie over to reveal **UBER** stamped in black on the reverse side.

"First time I ever saw that," she remarks.

"Donald," Dr. Nakamura says, "can you see this from where you're standing?"

"I can," Det. Chase says. "Me, too. Never saw a baggie stamped with the Uber trademark before."

"Then we are all in agreement." Dr. Nakamura carefully returns the baggie to the way he found it. "Now give me your impressions of the residue."

Det. Bishop steps closer to the vanity. "Looks like coke or heroin."

"My impression as well," he says.

"I'm leaning toward heroin," she says. "But the color looks a touch off."

Two evidence technicians appear outside the door.

"Gentlemen," Dr. Nakamura greets them. "Just give us a few more seconds, then she's all yours."

Det. Bishop exits the bathroom.

Dr. Nakamura pauses to take one last look around the bathroom. Then gathers his equipment and steps outside.

"All yours," he tells the evidence techs.

Dr. Nakamura and the two detectives start walking up the hallway.

"Donald," Det. Bishop says, "check out the living room. I'll take the bedroom as soon as I get back."

"Where you going?" Det. Chase asks.

"Downstairs. Want to talk to those two women outside. See if they can provide something of value."

"I'll walk out with you," Dr. Nakamura says.

They start walking.

"So, Ken," she says, "how are you going to handle this?"

"At least for now, I'm going to write it up as an apparent drug overdose, accidental. Other than the jewelry, which may or may not be meaningful, I don't see anything to contradict that assumption."

———

Dr. Nakamura and Det. Bishop exit the apartment building. Go separate ways. Dr. Nakamura walks toward the coroner's van. Det. Bishop heads toward the red Camaro.

The two dancers are standing behind the Camaro.

Det. Bishop displays her badge. "I'm Det. Bishop with the Delaware County C.I.D."

The dancers nod.

"I regret to inform you," she says, "that Miss Forsythe is deceased."

"Pretty much what we figured," Farrah says. "You know, when we saw the coroner's van show up."

"How are you acquainted with the deceased?"

"Work together," Farrah answers.

"Where?"

"Babes in Toyland," Farrah says, "on Columbus Boulevard."

"I see." Det. Bishop produces a small notebook. Opens it. Asks for names and contact information. Jots it all down, then asks, "How is it you came here today?"

"She didn't show up for her shift," Farrah says. "We tried calling and texting, but she didn't answer. She never misses work and she's never late. So our manager sent us to check on her."

"What's your manager's name?"

"Sam," Farrah replies. "Sam Cohen."

Det. Bishop jots his name in her notebook. "When was the last time either one of you saw her?"

"Last night at the club," Farrah says.

Det. Bishop looks at Candi.

"Same," Candi says.

"Do you have any idea how she left work?" Det. Bishop asks. "Or who she left with?"

Neither dancers knows.

CHAPTER 7

The next morning.

A mug of coffee's on my desk. Another episode of Better Call Saul's playing on the big screen. Suddenly, I hear someone knocking on my door.

I get up. Walk a few steps, open the door.

"Ah, My Friend."

"Saw your car outside," he says. "Figured you were home."

"Brilliant deduction, Watson."

"Ha-ha-ha." He fakes a laugh.

I'm on my way back to my desk by the time he closes the door and comes inside.

"Want something to drink?"

"Sure," he says.

"You know where it is."

Back at my desk. Open my laptop, go online. Hear him enter the kitchen. Hear him open the refrigerator door, start rooting around inside. After the door closes, I see him carrying a bottle of Canada Dry into the living room.

He takes a seat on the couch. "What're you watching?"

"Better Call Saul."

"Never seen it." He twists off the top, takes a sip. "What are you doing?"

"Trying to break this fucking code."

"What code?" he asks.

"Getting my first story published." I punch a number into my cellphone. "Hang on."

A recording answers. Five more punches before a female's voice finally says, "Ellery Queen. How can I help you?"

"I'd like to speak to your editor-in-chief."

"Is he expecting your call?" she asks.

"Does it make a difference?"

"Mr. Angelis doesn't accept random phone calls," she says. "What is the purpose of the call. Perhaps I can help you."

"Let's give it a try. I keep submitting stories. I think they're pretty good, but keep getting rejection slips."

"Are you published?" she asks.

"That's what I'm trying to do now."

"But are you *already* published?" she asks.

"No."

"That's a problem," she says. "Here at Ellery Queen we don't accept random submissions. We only deal with published writers."

"But that's not what it says on your website."

"I'm sorry for the confusion," she says. "But that *is* our policy."

I end the call, set the phone on the desk.

"Any luck?" My Friend says.

"Struck out swinging. But at least I found out why I keep getting rejections."

"So now what?" he asks.

"Hafta find a publication that deals with unpublished writers." Close my laptop, stand up. Pick up my coffee, move over to the couch. Take a seat next to My Friend. Stretch out my legs and prop my feet on the coffee table.

"Oh," he says. "Almost forgot. How'd it go with your stripper last night?"

"Different." I sip my coffee.

"How so?" My Friend asks.

"Actually talked to this one."

"No shit." He punks me a little. "Not afraid she might misconstrue something you say?"

"Good one. For you."

"Ha-ha-ha." Another fake laugh.

"She talked my ass off from the time I picked her up until I dropped her off."

"About what?" he asks.

"About blowing this guy and fucking that guy."

"Did sucking *your* cock ever enter the conversation?"

"No. But I helped her carry her things."

"Why?" he asks.

"She had a lot to carry and her wrist was sprained."

"One of these days that's going to get you in trouble."

"What is?"

"Helping people," he says.

"Do you know how ridiculous that sounds?"

"Hope I'm wrong," he says. "But it is possible."

"You're so wrong. But for your info, I also helped someone else last night." I purposely saved this for last.

"How?" he asks.

"Got a request when I was leaving the stripper's place. From a girl out on the Main Line."

"And?"

"And she's pissed at her boyfriend. Drinking wine all day. Long ride, all the way to Phoenixville. Listen to her problems. We do some bonding. Then she offers to buy me a drink. Right then and there."

"No shit," he says.

"Yep. So we have a couple drinks, and then wham-bam, thank you, ma'am."

"Get the fuck outta here," he says.

"Swear to God."

"You say she was pissed at her boyfriend?" he verifies.

"Yep."

"Sounds like a spite-fuck to me," he says.

"Some people might call it a spite-fuck. But I went online when I got home and did some research."

"You and your fucking research," he says.

I move back to my desk. Open my laptop, make a few clicks.

"Ah, here it is. And I quote, 'Transference is a psychiatric phenomenon that occurs when a patient suddenly redirects their feelings from a significant person in their life to the therapist.'"

"You're no therapist," he says.

"Ah, *Mon Amie*, but that's exactly who I was last night. I listened to her problems, *really* listened, and that's all psychiatrists do. They listen. Here's the best part. And, once again, I quote: 'This transference is often manifested as an erotic attraction towards their therapist.'"

"Interesting."

"Just like that, the boyfriend's out and I'm in."

"I feel honored," he says.

"How so?"

"I finally got to meet Sigmund Freud," he says.

"Good one, *Mein Freund*."

"Where'd you do her?" he asks.

"In the parking lot outside the bar. Standing up. Leaning against the car."

"Nobody saw you?" he says.

"After closing, nobody around. Moon shining down, stars twinkling up above, and I made her bark like a dog."

"You're not just a psychiatrist," he says. "You're also a poet."

"Thanks." I'm smiling.

"You shoulda made a video," he says, "and posted it on YouTube." He's laughing. "You going to see her again?"

"You're not going to believe this."

CHAPTER 8

The district attorney and his chief assistant prosecutor enter the main conference room at C.I.D. headquarters. Both wearing three-piece suits.

Robert Greene, 49, is the district attorney. Tall and lean, he goes by Bob around the courthouse.

Hank Baldino, 38, is the chief prosecutor. Originally from South Philly, he's short and stocky with dark wavy hair.

"Sorry we're late," the DA says.

"No problem, Bob," the chief replies. He's Herbert George, just turned 50. Always wears a shirt and tie, rarely a jacket, sleeves rolled up to the elbows. "We're still waiting for Frank."

The chief's sitting at the far end of a long conference table. Detectives Bishop and Chase are already seated on one side of the table. The prosecutor sits across from the detectives. And the DA takes a seat at the near end of the table.

Frank Santangelo arrives almost out of breath. He's 40, tall and stocky, a veteran of 19 years with the federal Drug Enforcement Agency.

"Sorry," he says. "Stuck in traffic on the Blue Route." Looks around. Spots the empty chair next to the prosecutor, takes a seat. "Ran all the way here from the garage."

"Thanks for being here," the chief begins. "I know this wasn't on anyone's agenda today. So I'll keep it as short as possible." Addresses Det. Bishop. "Pam, get us started."

"Yes, sir." She remains seated. "Yesterday, the body of a white female was found in the bathtub in her apartment at the Media Station Apartments. Pending any adverse findings in the subsequent autopsy, scheduled for Monday, her death's classified as an accidental drug overdose."

"Whoa," the DA interrupts. "Herb, you called us here to discuss an accidental overdose?"

"I understand your concern, Bob," the chief replies. "But please bear with us. The reason will soon become clear."

"Go ahead." The DA nods.

"Pam," the chief says, "please continue."

Det. Bishop taps the keypad in front of her and an image of the dead stripper appears on a large screen on the wall. "That's the victim," she says.

Everyone looks at the image for several seconds.

"Next," the chief says.

Det. Bishop taps again, and an image of the drug paraphernalia is superimposed off to the side of the victim. "We observed this drug paraphernalia," she continues, "in close proximity to the victim, along with a powdery white residue on the mirror, and a small plastic baggie next to the mirror."

"Looks exactly like your typical OD scene," the DA says. "Cocaine or heroin?"

"Ken couldn't be with us today," the chief says. "So he emailed us a copy of the drug analysis. Pam, do the honors."

She reads from her notebook. "Lab detected a lethal amount of $C_{22} H_{28} N_2 O$."

"What's that?" the DA asks.

"Fentanyl," the chief responds. "Please continue, Pam."

"This baggie's different than any we ever saw," she says.

"How so?" the DA asks.

She taps the keyboard to flip the image of the baggie to the reverse side. "This particular baggie is trademarked with the letters U-B-E-R stamped in black."

"Which is why Frank's here." The chief turns his head toward the DEA agent. "Frank, please take over."

"My pleasure," the DEA agent begins. "What we have here, gentlemen. Sorry, Pam. What we have here, *lady* and gentlemen, is the beginning of a fentanyl invasion into your jurisdiction."

"And we're hoping," the chief aims his response at the DA, "that if we take appropriate and proactive steps, and take them quickly, we might be able to nip its spread before it gains any traction."

"Please continue," the DA says.

"For two years," the agent continues, "my colleagues in New York have been surveilling an operation headed by a Mexican national calling himself the Cisco Kid." Glances at his notes. "Full name: Francisco Zayas. Big man in the Sinaloa Cartel with connections all the way back to Culiacán."

"El Chapo's group," the prosecutor throws in.

"Exactly," the agent says. "He controls nine drug cells in and around New York City. Right now, we have enough to indict him for conspiracy. But we want to bring him down hard, and bring down his whole ring along with him. So we're cooling our heels as we gather more and more intel."

"That's all well and good for you," the DA says, "but what's he got to do with us?"

"One of his products is fentanyl. He uses baggies stamped with the Uber trademark. Just like the one on the screen. And, get this, he uses Uber drivers to distribute his products."

"You don't say," the DA says.

"And, we believe, he sent one of his capos down here to set up a similar operation."

"What do you know about this operation?" the DA asks.

"Not much."

"That's why it's imperative," the chief says, "that we take appropriate and proactive steps quickly."

—

Two hours later.

Detectives Bishop and Chase enter the manager's office at the topless club. Introduce themselves and present their credentials.

"Please be seated." The manager indicates two chairs on the opposite side of his desk.

The detectives sit.

"Mr. Cohen," Det. Bishop begins, "we're doing some routine follow up on the death of one of your employees." Glances at her notebook. "Miss Rita Forsythe."

"I, uh, got the unfortunate news yesterday."

"Our condolences," Det. Bishop says. "What we're trying to do now is get an understanding about what happened. What can you tell us about her?"

"She was very, uh, popular with the customers. Shocking news. Definitely, uh, shocking. And all of us here at the club are willing to do whatever we, uh, can, to help you folks in your investigation."

"Thanks in advance for your cooperation," Det. Bishop says. "On her last night here, do you know what time she left the club? Who she left club with? Or how she left the club?"

"I know she left in an Uber because I ordered it for her. And I can provide someone who, uh, knows a little more." He presses a button on the intercom.

"Yes, sir," a female's voice replies.

"Roberta, please tell, uh, Sal to report to my office."

"Yes, sir."

A knock on the door comes almost immediately.

"Come in," the manager calls out.

The door opens, the bouncer enters. Stops just inside the door, closes it behind himself.

"This is, uh, Sal Mazza," the manager says. "He's one of our bouncers here and he, uh, was on duty that night."

"I'm Det. Bishop." She presents her credentials. "And this is my partner Det. Chase."

Det. Chase flashes his badge.

"We just told Mr. Cohen," Det. Bishop says, "that we're doing routine follow up on the death of Rita Forsythe."

The bouncer nods without saying anything.

"We'd like to ask you a question or two," she says.

"Do I need a lawyer?"

"Why?" Det. Bishop replies. "Did you do something wrong?"

"No," the bouncer says. "But that's what they always say on TV, ya know, on those cop shows." Nervous laugh. "Don't say anything without your lawyer being present."

"This isn't a cop show on TV," Det. Bishop says. "We're just trying to get some information. Do you understand?"

"Yeah."

"Good," she says. "Then let's try again. We're trying to determine Miss Forsythe's last movements on her last night here. Do we have your permission to proceed?"

"Yeah, sure," the bouncer says.

"Question number one. Do you know what time Miss Forsythe left the club?"

"Around 11:30."

"How can you be so sure?"

"That's when I took my break," he says. "I seen her putting on her coat. She left a few minutes later."

"I see," Det. Bishop says. "Do you know how she left the club?"

"She took an Uber."

"As I already mentioned," the manager interjects.

"Yes, sir," Det. Bishop says. "I remember." She looks at the bouncer. "It's Sal, is it not?"

"Yeah."

"Sal," Det. Bishop says, "to make sure I'm clear on this, you're telling me you saw Miss Forsythe leave here in an Uber. Is that correct?"

"Yeah."

"Did you see the vehicle she left in?"

"Silver SUV," he says. "But didn't catch the make."

"Did you see the driver?"

"White dude," he says. "Seen him load her things into the back of the SUV. But all I seen was his back."

"Any way you could identify him?"

"Never seen his face."

"What did the driver load into the SUV?"

"Her makeup kit," he says, "and some shopping bags. Like, from Macy's, I think. Two of them."

"Any idea what was in those shopping bags?"

"Clothes, I guess."

"Was she in the habit of taking an Uber home?"

"Most of them take Ubers," he says. "Uber or Lyft."

"Did she have a regular driver?"

"Not really," he says. "Somebody just shows up." A few seconds pass in silence. "You done with me yet?"

"Pretty much it." She gives her partner a look.

"By the way, Sal," Det. Chase says. "It is Sal, right?"

"Yeah."

"What happened to your face?" Det. Chase asks.

The question catches the bouncer off guard. Takes him two seconds to say, "I do judo."

"So you participate in judo?" Det. Chase asks.

"Yeah. I was doin' self-defense the other day. We were outside and people were just pickin' shit up off the ground, ya know, whatever they could find. My guy got, like branches from a weeping willow tree, and hit me across the face."

—

Rain's falling when the detectives exit the club.

"The judo routine didn't sound convincing," Det. Chase says. They're hurrying across the lot toward their unmarked car. "And he looked nervous as hell."

"For sure," Det. Bishop says. "But let's not lose focus of why we came here. Now we know she left here in an Uber."

"And we know," he adds, "she was found dead the next day with an Uber baggie in close proximity. Quite a coincidence."

They reach the car, get inside. Det. Chase behind the wheel. Det. Bishop riding shotgun.

Det. Bishop takes out her cellphone. Punches one of her speed dials, waits for an answer.

"Emily," she says as the car pulls away. "Pam here. Need you to contact Uber headquarters for us."

CHAPTER 9

Almost 8 o'clock when I pull off Lancaster Avenue and start heading up the driveway leading to the Radnor House.

Pass the main entrance, pull into a spot just around the bend. Take out my cellphone. Immediately hear a gentle tapping on the passenger's window. Dark outside, but just enough light to see Margo's face. She's smiling.

I lower the window. "Was just gonna call. Waiting long?"

"Just got here," she says, "and saw you pulling in."

"How'd you know it was me?"

"A girlfriend," she says with a flirtatious smile, "knows what kind of vehicle her boyfriend drives."

"Jess told you."

"And a lot more." Another one of those smiles.

"You got the advantage on me. Seems like you know more about me than I know about you. Other than you're quite pretty."

"Flattery will get you everywhere," she says. "Compliments come few and far between these days."

"Hard to believe. I'll meet you around back." I close the window. Exit the Envoy, meet her around back.

"You're right on time," she says.

"Out of character for me."

"How so?" she asks.

"When it comes to anything related to business, I make it a point to be early. But anything social, I don't give a shit when I get there. But in your case, I didn't wanta make you wait."

"Does that mean I'm business?" she asks. "Or should I consider myself special?"

Is it my imagination? Or is she flirting with me? "Special." I smile. "Now, changing the subject, I'm flipping coins."

"About what?" she says.

"No idea if we can pull off this boyfriend and girlfriend business."

"So I *am* just business," she says.

"You took that out of context."

"If you say so," she says.

"Here's what I was trying to say. Even if we *can* convince everyone that we're boyfriend and girlfriend, what do you get out of it? What do I get out of it? And what's the point of this whole masquerade?"

"By asking those questions," she says, "you already missed the point."

"Which is?"

"What does Jess get out of it?" she says.

"What *does* she get out of it?"

"In a nutshell," she says, "she's pissed at Pablo."

"Her boyfriend, right?"

"Right," she says. "She's suddenly hot for you, and wants to do some comparison shopping."

"So this is a meat market. The boyfriend and me hanging on racks, figuratively speaking?"

"Now you got it," she says.

"How do you feel about that? You know, being an integral part of the plot and all."

"I think it's hilarious," she says. "Jess is my best friend and I love her dearly. But if anyone else asked me to do something this stupid, I'd tell them to fuck off. Pardon my French."

"I know plenty of French."

"On the one hand," she says, "I refuse to believe this will work the way she thinks it will. Yet, on the other hand, I can't wait to see how it plays out. I mean, my sixth sense tells me it's not going to go smoothly."

"We'll find out soon enough. But I have a few questions, you know, things I'd know if we were–"

"Boyfriend and girlfriend?" Another smile. "Fire away."

"How'd we meet?"

"I called for an Uber one night," she says, "and you picked me up. Going from my place to The Grog."

"Perfect irony."

"Indeed," she says. "We started talking. You mentioned something about getting ready to quit for the night. I found you attractive, so I suggested quitting right then and there and joining me for a drink."

"Jess did tell you a lot."

"Sure did." Another one of those smiles. "You quit driving. We stopped for a drink, but you got a lot more than a drink."

"I'd like to find out more about that." My turn to flirt.

"I'd be disappointed if you didn't," she says.

"How old are you?"

"Jess and I are both 29," she says. "Known each other since kindergarten. We graduated from Phoenixville High, then she went to art school in Philly."

"What about you?"

"Graduated from Drexel," she says.

"So my new girlfriend's a genius."

"Not your stereotypical blonde," she says.

"Major?"

"Computer science," she says.

"You are a genius. Where do you work?"

"Comcast, in Center City," she says. "The new building. Programming software."

"Ever been engaged or married?"

"No to both," she says.

"Do you wanta get married?"

"You asking?" She stares at me with a straight face. But can't hold it for long, chuckles a little. "If I meet the right man, sure. Who doesn't?"

"And if you don't meet the right man?"

"I'm independent," she says. "I enjoy living by myself."

"What about kids?"

"Like I said," she says, "if I meet the right man, sure. Kids would be nice. If not, no big deal."

"Where do you live?"

"Radcliff House," she says. "Right around the corner on Conestoga Road."

"I know exactly where that is. Looks expensive."

"A one bedroom goes for $1,300," she says. "I can afford it, but hate paying that much for rent. Don't get me wrong, my unit's nice. But I'm thinking about buying a condo in Center City when the lease runs out. Where do *you* live?"

"Clifton Heights." She doesn't react. "You don't know where that is, do you?"

"Heard of it," she says.

"Other side of the tracks from you Main Liners."

She laughs. "I'm from Phoenixville, remember?"

"Almost forgot."

"My turn," she says. "Still need to know more about you."

"Shoot."

"Let's walk and talk." She starts leading the way. "Jess told me you're some sort of writer."

"Aspiring writer. Unfortunately, nothing published so far."

"What do you write about?" she asks.

"Mystery stories."

"I like mysteries," she says. "Are they sexy mysteries?" And she smiles.

"Not really. The magazines I'm trying for are G-rated."

"Too bad," she says. "I enjoy graphic sex." Another smile.

We reach the entrance, the glass doors open automatically. We enter.

A uniformed doorman steps up. "Good evening, Miss Margo," he says with a European accent. "Miss Jessika told me to expect you."

"Good evening, Fritz." Margo says.

"And your gentlemen companion." He looks at me.

"His name's Steve," she says.

"Pleasure to meet you, Mr. Steve." The doorman smiles.

"Steve," Margo says, "meet Fritz."

"My pleasure, Fritz."

The introductions complete, Margo leads the way across the lobby. We reach the elevators, she presses the button.

"How old are you?" she asks.

"Be 34 on my next birthday."

"Ever been engaged or married?" she asks.

"No."

"Do you want to?" she asks.

"You asking?" I smile.

The elevator arrives. The door opens, we step aboard.

"Nice twist" She presses the button for our floor.

"I'm normal. But for now, becoming a published writer is everything. That's the cake. Marriage and kids are the icing."

"Good luck," she says. "And I'm serious."

"Thanks. Do we need some sort of signal or password."

"For what?" she asks.

"In case our charade bombs and we hafta haul ass."

"Ah," she says. "A code word. Sure. Why not?"

"Any suggestions?"

"Just saw a rerun of Frasier last week," she says. "Rosie Perez was the guest star. You're familiar with the show, right?"

"Used to watch it with my mother all the time."

"So she was Frasier's blind date," she says. "Roz set it up, and gave them both code words. You know, in case one didn't like the other one."

"What were the code words?"

"Rosie's was super, and Frasier's was *enchanté*."

"Let's go with *enchanté*."

"Okay with me," she says.

A bell rings when the elevator reaches our floor.

"This is for good luck." I give her a quick kiss on the lips. Catch her by surprise. So much so, she's still staring at me when the elevator door opens.

"Same to you," she says. The look on her face tells me she's confused. Like she's wondering if the kiss meant anything.

"Which way?"

"Turn left," she says. "Last unit on the right."

I step off the elevator, wait for her. We turn left, start walking.

"You think we should hold hands?" she asks.

CHAPTER 10

Jess is squeezing a lime over a large bowl of guacamole. The lime's cut in half and she's squeezing by hand.

She sets the lime on a cutting board, starts mixing the guacamole with a large wooden spoon. Stops stirring after 20 seconds, licks the spoon. "Not bad."

She picks up the lime, squeezes out the last few drops. More mixing, another taste. "Just right."

She sets the lime on the cutting board, turns on the faucet. Rinses the wooden spoon. Sets it on the drain board, wipes her hands. Picks up the bowl and carries it into the living room.

Bon Jovi's "It's My Life" is playing at a volume set low enough to support normal conversation.

Jess places the guacamole on the coffee table, next to a platter of Buffalo wings, and in between bowls of nacho chips and potato chips. Artichoke dip and a platter of bread tidbits sit next to a large bowl of homemade salsa.

"Shredded chicken's almost ready," she announces.

The party's small in number. Jess's boyfriend Pablo and two couples. Ginger and Gary are married. Diane and Jim live together. All dressed casually in jeans and sweaters, except for Jess.

She's all in black. Looks sexy in an off-the-shoulder mesh top, skintight slacks, and spiked heels.

The doorbell rings.

"I got it." Jess starts walking toward the door.

Margo and I are holding hands when the door opens.

"This is Steve," Margo pretends to introduce me. "The man I've been telling you about."

"Pleased to meet you, Steve," Jess says.

"Likewise." I smile.

Margo gives me a quick kiss on the lips.

"I just put the food out," Jess says. "Come in."

We enter.

"You know everybody here," Jess tells Margo. She shuts the door. "Go in and introduce Steve. I've got one more dish in the oven."

—

Ten minutes later.

"Who Let the Dogs Out" starts playing.

I'm sitting at the dining room table with Gary, Jim, and Jess's boyfriend Pablo. We're sampling everything, drinking beer, and talking in between bites.

"What do you do?" Gary asks me.

"Drive for Uber. For now."

"And later?" Pablo asks.

"What's that?"

"You said you drive for Uber," Pablo says, "for now. What happens later?"

"Oh, that. My dream's being a mystery writer."

"No shit," Gary says. "That sounds cool."

"Not so cool right now. I'm still referred to as 'unpublished.' Still trying to break my cherry, but it's a bitch."

"Hang in there," Pablo says. "Anything worth doing comes with a price."

"Thanks. By the way, what do you do?"

"Own my own company," Pablo says. "A start-up. Making progress, slow but sure. So I can relate to your growing pains."

"What kind of company?"

"Software development," Pablo replies.

"What kind of software?"

"You ask a lot of questions," Pablo says.

"Comes with the territory. That's what writers do. That's how you learn shit. If it bothers you, I'll stop."

"No," Pablo says. "I get it. It's like this. I design proprietary software, using artificial intelligence, to collect and codify data."

"Sounds impressive. What kind of data?"

"Whatever kind my clients need."

"Careful," Gary warns me. "Show too much interest and he'll talk you into investing in his company."

"Is that right?"

"Jim and I are already investors," Gary says.

—

At the same time in the living room.

Diane and Ginger are sitting on the sofa. Margo and Jess are sitting in armchairs at opposite ends of the sofa. The chairs are turned to face the sofa to create a conversation area.

"How did you two meet?" Diane asks Margo.

"Called for an Uber one night," she answers, "and Steve showed up. You could say one thing just led to another."

"So he's an Uber driver," Jess plays along. "Interesting."

"For now." Margo smiles. "But he's not just an Uber driver. He wants to be a writer."

"What kind of writer?" Ginger asks.

"Mystery stories," Margo says.

"I like mystery stories," Diane says. "How old is he?"

"He'll be 34 on his next birthday."

"And good-looking," Diane says, "if you ask me."

"I think so." Margo smiles at Jess. "What do you think, Jess?"

"Too bad you saw him first," Jess says.

—

I take the last swallow from my bottle of Budweiser.

Jess calls out, "Steve, there's more beer in the refrigerator. Just help yourself."

"Thanks. Don't mind if I do."

I start walking with the empty, quickly reach the kitchen.

Back in the living room Jess stands up. "I better show him where it is."

"He can probably find the refrigerator on his own," Margo says.

"I'm sure he can," Jess replies. "But we recycle. I want to make sure the empty goes where it belongs."

I'm opening the refrigerator door when I feel two hands gripping the sides of my thighs from behind. I turn, find myself looking into Jess's eyes.

"I want you so bad," she whispers, starts kissing me.

I enjoy the affection for a good two seconds, pull back suddenly. "What about–?"

"We're safe," she whispers. "They're all busy out there."

"Hope you're right."

"It drove me crazy," she says, "when I saw you two holding hands." Then comes another quick kiss. "Even worse when I saw Margo kiss you."

Jess kisses me again.

On the one hand I'm enjoying this. But on the other hand I'm keeping one eye open. Staring at the doorway, hoping nobody walks in on us.

"I never did anything like this before," she says. Another quick kiss. "And the risk of getting caught is really turning me on. I'd like to do you. Right here on the floor. Right now."

—

At the same time in the living room.

"Anybody want a refill?" Margo asks.

"You flying?" Diane asks.

"That I am." Margo stands up. "What're you drinking?"

"Yellow Tail." Diane hands her empty glass to Margo.

"Ginger?" Margo asks.

"No thanks, I'm good."

Margo pivots, heads toward the kitchen carrying the two empty wine glasses.

I'm rounding the corner on my way out of the kitchen, almost bump into Margo. We come face to face.

"Almost a head on collision," Margo says. "Close enough for this." She kisses me on the lips. Not a long kiss, not a short kiss, but a kiss with a loud smacking of lips. "Did Jess teach you how to recycle?"

"Of course I did," Jess's voice comes from behind me. A second later she's standing right next to us. "That's why I put your empty in the blue bucket under the sink."

"Wasn't really paying attention." I give Margo a peck on the cheek, head back to where the guys are hanging out.

Margo continues into the kitchen.

Jess follows, catches up. Steps right in front of Margo, glares into her eyes. "What's your game?"

"What're you talking about?"

"All the kissing," Jess says. "I feel like wringing your fucking neck."

"We're just acting like boyfriend and girlfriend. Just like you asked us to. What's your problem?"

"Make sure it's just acting," Jess says. "No more kissing."

"Get over it. Your idea, not mine, remember? I'm just going with the flow."

"Whatever," Jess says.

"And speaking about acting." Margo sets the two empty wine glasses on the counter. "How about acting like a hostess. Two Yellow Tails, please."

"You know where it is." Jess gives Margo a dirty look, brushes past her on her way out of the kitchen.

Margo refills both glasses.

Moments later, Margo's back in the living room handing one of the glasses to Diane.

"Thank you," Diane says.

"Any time." Margo sips her wine. Raises her voice, "Jess, did you put in an application at that new place in Ardmore?"

"What new place?" Jess asks.

"Think it's called *Enchanté*."

CHAPTER 11

"What happened?" I ask Margo.

We're in the elevator on our way down to the first floor.

"Jess got bent out of shape because I kissed you," she says.

"Really? She started kissing me and said she wanted to do me right there on the kitchen floor."

"Too bad she didn't," Margo says.

"Why's that?"

"If I walked in," she says, "and found you two doing it on the floor, I would've made it a threesome before you two knew which end was up."

"Sounds interesting."

"Sure does," she says. "But that's not the way it went with us. She followed me into the kitchen and said she wanted to ring my fucking neck."

"That *is* a little different."

"But I predicted this was going to happen," she says. "My sixth sense knew things weren't going to go smoothly."

"Pretty much inevitable."

"How so?" she asks.

"To begin with, we look the part of boyfriend and girlfriend."

"We *do* look the part." Margo smiles.

"And we played our parts well. So if she's so hot for me, like you insist, our kissing's going to make her jealous. Now let me ask you a question."

"Sure."

"You're gorgeous. Why no boyfriend?"

"Long story," she says.

"I don't have a curfew."

The bell rings. We step off the elevator, begin walking across the lobby.

"Leaving so soon, Miss Margo?" the doorman asks.

"Work tomorrow, Fritz," she says. "Have to get up early."

"Then good evening to you, Miss Margo."

"Good evening to you, Fritz," she says. "See you next time."

"And nice to meet you, Mr. Steve. Hope to see you again."

"Likewise, Fritz."

We reach the exit, the door opens automatically. We step outside, take a few steps. Stop, look at each other.

"Do you?" I ask.

"Do I what?"

"Hafta go to work tomorrow?"

"No," she says. "Just didn't want to prolong the conversation."

"Then let's hear your long story about why you don't have a boyfriend."

"Okay." She takes my hand and leads me toward our parked cars. "I caught the prick cheating on me, so I dumped him."

"When was that?"

"Five months ago," she says. "What about you?"

"Already told you. No time for relationships right now."

"So you haven't had a girlfriend for how long?" she asks.

"Well, my last legitimate girlfriend was, um, two years ago. Beautiful girl. She's talking about getting married, having kids, and buying a house in the suburbs."

"What happened?" she asks.

"I had a real job back then. Territory manager for a large textile manufacturer. Did a lotta traveling. Anyway, took a business trip to Albany during the summer. While I'm gone, she goes down to Long Beach Island."

"Why there?" she asks.

"Her parents are rich. Own a mansion on the beach."

"And?"

"And one of my buddies goes to the Tiki Bar one night. Very popular place on LBI. And he sees her dancing with some guy. Next thing he knows they're all over each other, right there on the dance floor. Kissing and shit. So he calls me."

"You're still in Albany?" she asks.

"Asleep in my hotel room. But he wants me to know right away. So when I get back home I confront her. She admits it. She's sorry, oh, so sorry. Got drunk. Didn't know what she was doing. Never happen again. Please forgive her. You know, all that happy horseshit."

"Did you buy any of it?" she asks

"No fucking way. No way I could ever trust her after that. Don't need drama like that in my life."

"Well you got a triple-header right now," she says.

"How's that?"

"To begin with," she says, "there's Jess and Pablo. Then we have Jess and you. And now add in me and you."

"Why me and you?"

"We're supposedly on a date," she says, "right?"

"We're pretending to be on a date."

"*Are* we pretending?" she asks. "I don't know about you, but I'm not pretending anymore."

"You're not?"

"I not only find you attractive," she says, "but sexy as hell. Then add in the fact I'm horny as hell because I haven't been with a man in the last five months."

CHAPTER 12

The next morning.

Jess is stepping out of the shower after toweling off. Slips into a pair of sexy white panties from Victoria's Secret. Next comes a tank top, also white, and bare midriff.

Stretches her arms in the air, takes a deep breath. Lowers her arms. Walks out of the bedroom, down the hallway toward the living room.

She finds the drapes drawn to block sunlight from streaming through the sliding doors. Sees Pablo sitting on the sofa. He's wearing a Sixers sweatshirt, blue bikini briefs, and black anklets. Holding an Xbox controller, playing some NBA game on the big-screen TV.

She sees his jeans tossed on the floor next to a pair of LeBron James sneakers. She pivots without saying a word, returns to the bedroom.

A few moments pass.

She returns carrying a pillow. Advances toward the sofa quickly and quietly, swats Pablo in the back of the head with the pillow. The swing's not meant to be a knockout blow, but not a love tap either. Hard enough to make him drop the controller onto the sofa.

"What the fuck?" Pablo says.

"Dick!"

"Can't you see I'm in the middle of a game?" He picks up the controller, goes back to the game.

"You're a dick."

"First you swat me with a goddam pillow." Never takes his eyes off the TV screen. "And now you're calling me names. What the fuck's going on?"

"Like you don't know."

"No, I don't know." He keeps looking at the screen, keeps playing the game. "You're lucky I'm not a violent man."

"Why? What would you do? Kill me?"

"You never know," he says.

"We need to talk."

He keeps playing the game.

"All you do is play games." She moves between Pablo and the TV screen, does an enticing pirouette. "How about playing a game with me?"

"Hang on." He tries to look around her. "Almost halftime."

"We don't need to wait until halftime. The way you play *my* game, you can get back to *your* game before halftime."

"Very funny," he says.

"You know, I had positive expectations last night."

"About what?" He finally takes a break from the game.

"About a man and a woman having sex. There was a party here last night. Plenty of alcohol flowing. Yet nothing happened. You never even came into the bedroom. I can't remember the last time we did it. You got something going on the side?"

"I refuse to qualify that with an answer."

"It's, like, you place no value on our relationship."

Pablo doesn't respond.

"Well?" she asks. "Do you?"

"You know I do."

"I'm not so sure anymore. You certainly don't show it."

"That's nonsense," he says.

"Do you love me?"

"I refuse to qualify that with an answer."

"A simple yes or no will do."

He doesn't answer.

"When we first started going out," she says, "everything progressed smoothly. I fell in love with you, and believed you loved me, too. I could see a natural progression. Love. Marriage. Children. Happily ever after till death do us part."

"And you don't see that anymore?"

"No.

"You're way off."

"Prove it." She strikes another sexy pose. "Do me right now. Right here on the sofa. Or on the floor for crying out loud. I don't care where. Your choice. Just do me right now."

"Can't."

"Why not?"

"What time is it?" he asks.

"What difference does that make?"

"I have an appointment," he says, "with some prospective investors. Trying to put a deal together."

"What kind of deal?"

"Don't worry your pretty little head," he says

"*Don't worry your pretty little head*," Jess imitates his words with emphasis and disdain. "*Don't worry your pretty little head*. That's all you say anymore. We've been together for almost a year now, but I still have no idea what makes you tick."

"Don't worry your pretty little head," he says.

"See what I mean. I don't even know where you stay when you're not here."

"You know where I live," he says.

"All I know is what you told me. Somewhere between Kensington and Fishtown. But you never took me there, and I never set one foot inside your door."

"Told you a million times–" he starts to say.

"Yeah-yeah. Bad neighborhood. Crime and drugs."

"That's the way it is," he says, "and I don't want anything to happen to you."

"Bullshit. I'm a big girl. Willing to take my chances."

"Well I'm not," he says.

"And you still neglected to come up with a plausible explanation for ignoring me on the day I got fired. You just fucking ignored me."

"I told you what happened," he says. "Meeting some new investors about some new software aimed at sports betting. Designed to enhance their chances of winning and maximizing their profits."

"Bullshit."

"Look," he says. "I go to work every goddam day. Busting my ass to become the best software developer around, because I'm trying to make enough money so you never have to work another day in your life."

"I never asked you to do that."

"All I ask in return," he says, "is that you show a little understanding, instead of nagging me all the time."

"You think I nag you?"

"That's all you do," he says. "That's all you've been doing since you walked in here and hit me over the head with that goddam pillow. You're, like, all you do is play video games. You never do me anymore. You never let me stay at your place. You never this. You never that. Just one nag after another."

"Really? Is that the way you see it?"

"Exactly the way I see it," he says.

"Fine. Then from now on, do whatever the fuck you want. Play your stupid fucking games until the fucking cows come the fuck home. But play them somewhere else. I'm done."

"What are you talking about?" he says.

"I'm done with you. I don't deserve this. I deserve somebody who gives a shit about me. But you don't, and I'm not spending one more second of my life with such an inconsiderate dick. So pack up your shit, dick. Pack up your precious game. Get the fuck out, and stay the fuck out."

CHAPTER 13

Margo's holding the corpse pose. Totally relaxed. Oblivious to the four women lying on yoga mats in close proximity to her. All holding the same pose.

Also oblivious to Jess.

Jess is standing on the sidewalk outside the yoga studio. Watching through a large plate-glass window. Waiting for the class to end.

Five minutes pass before Margo ends the pose.

She picks up her towel, gets up on her feet. From a male perspective, she's looking hot in black yoga pants, skintight, and a white halter top trimmed in black.

Another minute to gather her purse. Puts on her jacket, heads for the exit.

"You fucked him," Jess shouts as soon as Margo steps outside. "Didn't you?"

The words hit Margo's ears before she sees Jess.

Margo turns. "Here? You're going to pull that shit right here?" She starts walking toward her vehicle.

Jess follows right behind.

"What's wrong with right here?" Jess shouts.

Margo stops. Wheels around, goes face-to-face with her best friend. "*Il faut laver son linge sale en famille.*"

"What the fuck's that supposed to mean?"

"Napoleon's words," Margo says. "Way back in 1815. And they still hold true today."

"Sorry. I never learned French."

"You would have," Margo says, "if you went to a real school instead of a stupid fucking art school."

People are stopping, staring at the spectacle suddenly unfolding in front of them.

"Since you're so fucking smart," Jess says, "clue me in on what that's supposed to mean."

"Literally translated, 'You have to wash your dirty clothes with your family.' But here in the U.S., we modify it for you non-French speakers." Raises her voice until she's shouting. "Don't air your dirty laundry in public."

Margo turns, starts walking away again.

Jess grabs Margo's right wrist, won't let go.

Margo tries to shake her arm free. Keeps walking, winds up pulling Jess along behind. They proceed like that all the way to Margo's black Escalade.

Margo stops, spins around to face Jess. "Are you going to let go? Or do I have to punch your fucking lights out?"

"Let's talk about this." Jess releases Margo's wrist.

"Nothing to talk about."

Margo digs a set of keys out of her purse. Beeps the driver's door to unlock it. Gets inside, starts the engine.

Jess steps in front of the Escalade, presses her chest against the grill. "Run me over." Jess turns toward the crowd and yells, "Hit and run. You're all my witnesses."

Margo lowers the driver's window. "Get in."

Jess runs around to the passenger door, gets inside.

Margo pulls away, exits the lot onto Lancaster Avenue. "Thanks to you," Margo says, "I'll never be able to show my face in there again."

"Puts us in the same boat."

"Okay," Margo says. "You want to talk, so talk."

"Why'd you do it?"

"Do what?" Margo asks.

"Don't play dumb with me. I know you fucked Steve. Why?"

"Uh, let's see," Margo says. "To begin with, I was horny as a toad. And I was on a date with a man. No, make that a man I find both handsome and quite sexy."

"You were on a *pretend* date."

"Maybe when it started." Margo starts making a right turn onto a side street. "But that sure ain't how it ended, sister." Pulls into a vacant spot and parks.

"I saw him first."

"Big fucking deal," Margo says. "You have a boyfriend."

"Not anymore."

"You broke it off with Pablo?" Margo asks.

"Threw his ass out an hour ago. But now we have a problem, you and me. You just fucked the man I want to marry."

"You met him one day before me," Margo says.

"But I really like him."

"So do I," Margo says. "What am I supposed to do?"

"You were only with him for one night."

"So were you," Margo says.

"End it with Steve. This fling. Whatever you want to call it."

"Screw you," Margo says. "Who the fuck are you to issue an ultimatum? Maybe you're not the only one who has dreams about getting married and starting a family."

"You never said anything like that before."

"I wore that mask well," Margo says. "Way I see it, he's up for grabs."

"Fuck you." Jess opens the door, gets out of the Escalade. "You're not worth the aggravation."

She slams the door, walks away.

CHAPTER 14

That night.

I'm at the Springfield Country Club watching My Friend wrestle Cry Baby Waldo.

Cry Baby Waldo is a gigantic man, dressed in pink from head to toe. Pink wife-beater undershirt. Pink tights. Pink shoes. And pink socks with pink bows.

My Friend's wearing a black Speedo. He's muscular, 6-feet tall, a little over 200 pounds.

Cry Baby Waldo lifts My Friend up, onto his shoulders. Extends his arms upward, hoists My Friend over his head. Thus begins the classic airplane-spin maneuver. Cry Baby Waldo circles the ring, looking for the perfect spot to body slam My Friend.

The auditorium's full.

I'm sitting ringside in the midst of screaming fans.

"Slam his ass," shouts the guy on my right.

"No-no-no," pleads a woman behind me. "He's too pretty."

Cry Baby Waldo body slams My Friend. He lands with a vicious thud. So vicious, it makes my seat quiver.

My Friend lays in the middle of the ring. Showman that he is, he pretends to writhe in pain. Eyes closed. Looks as helpless as a lamb about to be slaughtered.

Cry Baby Waldo's climbing the ropes in the corner of the ring. Not easy for a man who weighs 350 pounds. His weight keeps shifting back and forth, making the ropes wobble uncontrollably.

I'm wondering if he's going to make it, or fall on his fat ass.

Somehow he's standing erect, straddling the top rope. Left foot on one side of the turnbuckle. Right foot on the other side. Extends his arms outward like a tightrope walker using a balance pole. Holds that pose for several seconds.

Bends his knees until he's crouching like a baseball catcher. Pushes off the top ropes with both legs. Sends 350 pounds of beef flying through the air with no safety net below.

No doubt he's gonna crash-land right on top of My Friend.

An ominous hush falls over the crowd.

My Friend knows what's coming. Also knows when it's coming. Opens his eyes, sees Cry Baby Waldo soaring toward him. Makes a face like he's panic stricken, rolls out of the way just in time.

Cry Baby Waldo belly flops onto the mat. So hard, the first three rows of spectators feel the vibrations.

My Friend rolls Cry Baby Waldo onto his back, pins his shoulders to the mat.

The referee flops down on his hands and knees. Pounds out the count with his right hand. "One! Two! Three!"

My Friend jumps to his feet.

The referee raises My Friend's right arm in the air. Hit Man Bruno wins the match.

All eyes go to straight to Cry Baby Waldo lying in the middle of the ring. Rolls over onto his stomach. Starts pounding his hands and feet on the mat. Squealing like a baby throwing a temper tantrum. Sucking his thumb.

His manager tosses a king-sized plastic baby bottle into the ring. Cry Baby Waldo picks up the bottle, starts sucking on the giant nipple.

The crowd goes wild with laughter.

—

An hour later.

Four of us are sitting at a table next to the windows in the dining room at Pinocchio's restaurant in Media.

Showered and dressed, Cry Baby Waldo and My Friend are sitting on one side of the table. I'm sitting on the other side with a guy named Joe. He's part of the management team at ECWA.

My Friend's drinking an Amaretto sour. Cry Baby Waldo and Joe are drinking glasses of draft beer. I'm drinking a bottle of Bud, no glass.

"Gotta hurt when you land like that," I say to Waldo.

"Crushes the fuckin' wind right outta ya. Makes it tough to breathe. But ya learn fast. Spread out and hit with as much of your body as possible. Spreads the impact."

"Here comes the pizza," Joe says.

"About fuckin' time," Cry Baby Waldo says. "I'm hungry–"

"Yeah-yeah-yeah," My Friend finishes his thought. "We know. Heard it a million times. Hungry enough to eat a horse."

The waitress sets a large rectangular pizza in the middle of the table. A large Sicilian, half plain, half pepperoni.

"Just wave if you need anything else," she says, walks away.

Cry Baby Waldo's digging into the pizza with both hands. One slice loaded with pepperoni goes onto his plate. Another slice goes halfway into his mouth with one push.

Joe grabs a plain.

My Friend's using the spatula to politely place a plain slice onto his plate.

I'm awaiting my turn when my cellphone rings. Dig it out of my pocket before the third ring. "Hello."

It's Jess. "You busy?"

"Just having a pizza with the guys."

"I'd like to get together with you," she says.

"Love to. When and where?"

"Where are you now?" she asks.

"At Pinocchio's in Media. Know where it is?"

"I do. Be there soon."

Cry Baby Waldo's chewing his pizza like the end of the world's in sight. Joe's chewing like a normal person. But My Friend's sitting there content to watch me on the phone.

I end the call.

"Who was that?" My Friend asks.

"Girl from the other night."

"Your rider?" he asks.

"Yep."

"You do Uber, too?" Cry Baby Waldo wipes his mouth with the back of a meaty hand.

"Yep."

"The one you nailed?" My Friend asks.

"Right."

"Did I just hear ya right?" Cry Baby Waldo reaches for another slice of pizza. "You screwed one of your riders?"

I'm grinning with pride in front of these macho guys.

"How'd that happen?" Waldo takes a big bite of his pizza.

"Believe it or not," I say, "it was her idea. I was just lucky enough to be in the right place at the right time."

"My man," Waldo says. "Up high."

I reach across the table and we slap hands.

"What's she look like?" Joe asks.

"See for yourself. She'll be here in a few minutes."

CHAPTER 15

The Sicilian's gone.

I'm on my second bottle of Bud. Cry Baby Waldo and Joe are on their third draft. My Friend's drinking another Amaretto sour on the rocks.

Under ordinary circumstances they woulda left as soon as the pizza was gone. But they're curious to see the rider I screwed.

The door opens, here she comes.

I stand up, wave her over.

She starts moving in our direction. Looking good in a form-fitting navy windbreaker and skin-tight grayish leggings.

"I see you found it all right," I say.

"Been here a couple times." She kisses my cheek, then I introduce her to the guys.

The booth behind us is vacant. I pick up my beer. Pivot, place the bottle on that table. Then Jess and I sit across from each other.

The waitress comes right over. "Would you like a menu?"

"No thanks," Jess says. "Just bring me what he's drinking."

"Okay," the waitress says. "Be right back."

"Wait," Jess says before the waitress gets away. "I'll take a shot of Cuervo." She looks at me. "Shot?"

"Why not? Make it two."

"Two it is." The waitress walks away.

"I apologize," Jess says.

"For what?"

"Making you and Margo pretend to be boyfriend and girlfriend like that. It was a bad idea."

"Glad you remember it was *your* idea."

"I admit it," she says. "Let's just say it was an experiment that, well, that didn't turn out the way I expected."

"What *did* you expect?"

"Looking back," she says, "not so sure. But I never expected you two to play your parts so well."

"Guess I shoulda been an actor."

"Okay, Mr. Bradley Cooper," her tone changes dramatically, "out of curiosity, exactly how well did you play your part?"

"What're you talking about?"

"You two left in quite a rush," she says.

"Margo said you two got into some sort of argument. You know, because she kissed me. Said you threatened to wring her fucking neck."

"I did get a little carried away," she admits.

"So she wanted to leave."

"Pretty early when you left," she says.

"Wasn't like we planned to leave early."

"When exactly did you plan to leave?" she asks.

"We never discussed it. Only met her ten minutes before we got to your place, out in the parking area. Barely got to talk. Just a little in the elevator on the way up. We planned to socialize at the party and leave when it was over."

"Leave and go where?" she asks.

"We never discussed it."

"How *did* you two leave?" she asks.

"We got there in two cars and we left in two cars."

"Did you go your separate ways?" she asks. "Or did you two, you know, go somewhere?"

"What do you mean?"

"You know exactly what I mean," she says. "Did anything happen between you and Margo after you left?"

"Like what?"

"You know," she says, "like what happened between you and me?"

I look away. Stalling. Wanting the questions to end.

"Did you fuck her?" she blurts out.

Obviously I know the answer. But I'm looking for a way to weasel out of this. I glance over Jess's shoulder, see three faces hanging on every word.

"Well?" she demands.

"Umm–" Stalling and looking at the guys at the same time. They signal me not to say anything.

"You did," she says, "didn't you? I know you fucked my best friend. I just want to hear you admit it."

"Umm–"

All three guys are mouthing warnings. I can read their lips. *Don't say shit. Keep your mouth shut. Shut the fuck up.*

"Save the bullshit excuses," she says. "You're bigger than that. Like I said, I take the blame. But I know you fucked her. So where do we stand now?"

"Where did we stand before? You have a boyfriend."

The guys are shaking their heads. Still giving me signs to clam up. Jess must see my eyes wandering, glances over her shoulder and catches them watching.

"Excuse me." She waits for them to look away before turning her attention back to me. "I thought something clicked between us."

The waitress arrives carrying our drinks on a tray. Sets a bottle of Budweiser and a glass in front of Jess, shots of tequila in front of both of us.

"Thanks," I tell the waitress.

"If you need anything," she says, "just wave."

"Now where was I?" Jess continues. "Oh, yeah. I was thinking about, well, thinking about you and me, and what the future holds."

"I thought you were in a committed relationship."

"Really?" she says. "Did you think I was in a committed relationship when you were fucking me?"

"To me, it seemed like two consenting adults."

I glance over Jess's shoulder. The guys' eyes are all over me once again. Now they're grinning, giving me the thumbs-up.

"For your information," she says, "I dumped Pablo today, and I was hoping that you and–"

"Whoa, Jess. Stop right there. No way I can fit a serious relationship into my life right now."

"And I'm telling you," she says. "Right here and right now. I'm going to do everything in my power to change your mind."

"Then it's all on you. Forewarned is forearmed."

"Let's drink to that." She picks up her shot glass.

"Let's say I drink this shot. Does that imply any sort of obligation or commitment on my part?"

"No strings," she says.

I pick up the shot glass.

"To many happy days ahead," she says.

We tap glasses, throw the tequila down in quick swallows. Jess waves at the waitress.

"Two more shots, please."

CHAPTER 16

Early the next morning, Sunday, at the Media Station Apartments.

Detectives Bishop and Chase are sitting behind a desk inside the manager's office.

His name's Denny. A skinny hipster, around 30, with a man-bun and scruffy beard. He's scrolling through his computer looking for the surveillance video from the night in question.

"Don't tell me you erased it," Det. Bishop says.

"Relax," the hipster says. "Ah, here it is."

"Start around midnight," Det. Bishop says.

The hipster fast forwards the video, pauses. "Check it out." He swings the monitor around, hits **PLAY**. The video's clear enough to see a tall brunette approaching the entrance to a building.

"That her?" Det. Bishop asks.

"Hang on." The manager pauses the video. Leans around to get a better look at the monitor. "Yeah, that's her."

"Can you zoom?" Det. Bishop asks.

"No problem." He zooms closer on her face, freezes the screen. "Close enough?"

"Perfect," Det. Bishop says.

Both detectives take a good look. "Now keep going," she says.

The manager hits **PLAY**. A white male comes into view carrying a makeup case and two shopping bags.

—

An hour later.

Detectives Bishop and Chase are sitting in a conference room at C.I.D. headquarters with Chief George. Watching the same surveillance video on a big screen on the wall.

The tall brunette comes walking into view.

"That the victim?" the chief asks.

"It is," Det. Bishop says.

A white male comes into view.

"That the suspect?" the chief asks.

"We believe it is," Det. Bishop says.

"What's he carrying?" the chief asks.

"The bouncer," she says, "told us she left the club carrying a makeup case and two shopping bags."

"Sure looks like a makeup case," the chief says, "and two shopping bags."

"He also told us he saw the Uber driver load those items into the back of his vehicle."

"Is that the Uber diver?"

"Emily contacted Uber headquarters," Det. Bishop says. "She obtained the identity of the driver. Name's Steve Piasecki. And Uber keeps recent face shots of all their drivers on file."

She clicks the computer keyboard, zooms in on the man's face on the video. Pauses the video. Makes three clicks, superimposes the driver's file photo right next to the face on the video.

"What do you think?" she asks.

"Looks like the same guy to me," the chief says.

"Now watch this," she says.

She starts the video again. The brunette leads the white male up several steps to the entrance. She opens the door, holds it open. The white male enters the building carrying the makeup case and shopping bags. She follows him inside, closes the door.

"That definitely places the suspect inside the building," the chief says. "Do you have a video that places him inside her apartment?"

"Unfortunately we do not." Det. Bishop stops the video. "No interior cameras at Media Station."

"Review what we have," the chief says.

"One, we have an Uber driver transporting the victim home. Two, she's found dead the next day of an apparent drug overdose. Three, the driver's the last person seen with her. Four, we have a drug baggie in close proximity to the victim. Five, it's stamped with the Uber logo. And six, we have a video with the victim and the Uber driver entering her building together."

"Looks like we found us a drug dealer."

CHAPTER 17

A bottle of tequila and two shot glasses are sitting on a bedside table. Bottle's almost empty.

It's a little after noon and Jess and I are in bed together. Halfway on top of each other. Breathing heavy and perspiring. I catch my breath, take the end of the sheet and wipe a few drops of perspiration from my forehead.

"You're pretty good at this," she says.

"Done it a few times before."

I roll onto my back.

She cuddles up next to me.

A TV's sitting on top of a bureau just past the foot of the bed. An episode of The Blacklist is playing.

"Police! Open up!"

"Is that the TV?" Jess says.

I lift my head, look at the screen. Don't see any police action.

"Police! Open up!" Now comes a loud pounding on my front door. "Police! Open up!"

"What the fuck." I kick off the covers, roll out of bed. Pick up my tee-shirt and undershorts from off the floor. Put them on quickly. "Hold on, I'm coming."

Jess is looking at me.

"Get dressed while I find out what's going on."

I shuffle out of the bedroom, walk down the hallway to the front door. Open the door, see a white male and a white female standing in the hallway. No idea who they are or why they're knocking on my door.

"Steve Piasecki?" the female asks.

"Yep."

"I'm Det. Bishop." She displays a badge, tilts her head in the male's direction. "And this is Det. Chase."

He flashes a badge.

"We're with the Delaware County C.I.D.," she says.

I'm both surprised and confused. "What can I do for you?"

"We'd like a few minutes of your time," she says. "Just, you know, to go someplace and talk."

"About what?"

"Concerning Miss Rita Forsythe," she says.

The name doesn't ring a bell. "Who?"

"We contacted Uber headquarters," she explains, "and understand you picked up Miss Rita Forsythe two nights ago. At the Babes in Toyland topless club on Columbus Boulevard."

"Oh, right. Must be the stripper's real name."

"Correct," she continues. "And from there, you transported her to the Media Station Apartments. Is that correct?"

"Yep. But what's this all about it? Did something happen?"

"You could say that," her partner says.

"Is this about the bouncer?"

"That's what we're trying to clear up," she says.

———

Half an hour later inside a small Interrogation Room at C.I.D. headquarters.

I'm sitting on one side of a small table.

The two detectives are sitting on the opposite side.

"Just tell us what happened," the male detective says, "and you're free to go."

"No problem. Picked her up at Babes in Toyland on Columbus Boulevard, and then I drove her home."

"We already know that," the female detective says. "Now we're trying to get a better understanding of what happened between you two."

"Nothing happened. I drove her home. That's my job. And then I dropped her off. That's it."

"Are you involved with her?" she asks.

"Whatta ya talking about?"

"Romantically," the male follows up. "You know, are you sexually intimate with her?"

I laugh out loud.

"What's so funny?" he asks.

"I never saw her before she came out of the club and started walking toward my vehicle. Plus, I'd never get involved with a stripper in the first place."

"Why not?" he says. "You a fag?"

I laugh again.

"Did I say something funny?" he asks.

"Nothing you said so far is funny."

"I'm not trying to be funny," he says.

"You're succeeding quite well." Suddenly I realize they're working on some sort of hidden agenda. "Look, I'm done talking."

"But we're not done talking to you," he says. "*We* tell *you* when you're done talking."

"When this chitchat started, you wanted me to tell you what happened and then I was free to go. So I told you what happened, but that wasn't good enough. Now you're trying to hard-ass me. This is bullshit. I'm gonna remain silent from this point on. I wish to speak with a lawyer."

"Look, Steve," her voice is suddenly full of compassion, "we're just talking among ourselves."

"You know," the male detective interjects, "man to man."

"So let's just keep talking," she says. "Once lawyers come into the picture, everything turns into a shit storm. Things turn confrontational."

"And when things turn confrontational," he says, "we start playing hardball. We book you to get what we need?"

"You don't want that, Steve," she says. "Do you?"

—

"My Friend." I'm still alone inside the same Interrogation Room, talking on my cellphone. "Thank God you answered."

"I always answer."

"Bullshit. But I don't have time to argue."

"You Ubering?" he asks.

"I wish. Look, I need a favor."

"Like what?"

"I'm in jail."

"Ha-ha-ha." Fakes a laugh. "Seriously, where are you?"

"No shit. I'm in fucking jail."

"You serious?" he asks.

"Yep."

"Why?"

"No fucking clue. Was in my apartment an hour ago. In bed with Jess."

"Nice."

"Yeah-yeah. Please. Just listen."

"Go ahead."

"Someone started pounding on my door. Works out it was these two detectives. Said they just wanted to talk to me. But they drove me down here to the courthouse in Media and started questioning me."

"About what?"

"Something musta happened to that stripper. Because once they got me down here, they started asking questions about her. Still have no idea what this is all about. They won't tell me shit, and now they're pretty much holding me against my will."

"What're you going to do?"

"That's why I called you. I need a fuckin' lawyer."

—

Detectives Bishop and Chase are sitting in the chief's office.

"So what's his story?" the chief asks.

"He admits to picking her up and driving her home," Det. Bishop says. "But now he quit talking and asked for a lawyer."

"I know he's a drug dealer," Det. Chase says. "He's got that look. I think we can turn the heat up and get him to spill his guts. Then we can find out where the shit's coming from."

"That would be nice," the chief says. "But everything sounds circumstantial so far."

"Yes, sir, it is," Det. Chase agrees. "But we'll get enough to hold him."

"On what?" the chief asks.

"Reasonable suspicion," Det. Chase says.

"Reasonable suspicion of what?" the chief asks.

"Possession," Det. Chase says, "intent to distribute, and sales. You name it, he did it. With a little pressure, we'll get him to give it all up."

"Where does it stand now?" the chief asks.

"We let him make a phone call," Det. Bishop says.

"On one of our lines?" the chief asks.

"No. His cellphone."

"So we don't really know," the chief says "if a lawyer's going to show up, or not. Good. He's not under arrest. We don't have to provide him with a public defender. Squeeze him. See if you can get him to crack."

—

I'm sitting in exactly the same place in the Interrogation Room.

The door opens, the detectives return.

The female takes a seat across from me.

The male remains standing.

"Listen, Steve," she begins, "we're trying to help you."

I laugh out loud.

"You think that's funny?" Her partner takes a step toward me in an aggressive manner. "You're a wise ass, aren't ya?"

"Relax, Donald," she tells her partner. "I'll handle this."

He backs off.

"We can get some of your charges reduced," she says.

I glare at her. "What charges?"

"Just tell us who your supplier is," she says, "and we'll go to bat for you. We'll protect you."

"Stop right there," comes a man's voice in stern tones.

My eyes shoot toward the door.

A man's standing in the doorway. Looks to be around 50, three-piece suit, holding a briefcase.

"Come on, guys," he tells the detectives. "You can't talk to my client when I'm not in the room. You know better than that."

"We didn't know Mr. Piasecki had retained representation," she says.

"Now you do." He points toward the door. "So hit the pike."

She gets up slowly, she and her partner leave.

He waits for them to shut the door. Looks directly into my eyes. "Bernard Wald, Esquire, at your service. Your friend Mike informed me you were in some sort of jam and needed a lawyer."

"My Friend came through." I get up on my feet. "Thank goodness."

We shake hands.

"Have you been interviewed yet?" he asks.

"Yes, sir. Twice. First time about an hour ago. Then they let me call My Friend, uh, Mike. They came back two minutes ago and started playing good cop, bad cop."

"Feel free to drop the sir," he says. "Bernie works fine."

"Yes, sir." I chuckle. "Yes, Bernie."

"Much better," the lawyer says. "I have a lot of experience working with this pair. They're usually square shooters."

"She was the good cop. He was the one hard-assing me."

"I get the picture," he says. "But bear this in mind. They're real good detectives. If given the right opportunity, they *will* nail your ass to the cross."

"I understand."

"So don't help them," he says.

"I understand."

"Did they Mirandize you yet?" he asks.

"No."

"Good," he says. "So if you let anything slip, it's inadmissible."

"Bernie, I don't have anything to let slip."

"Then, please, tell me what this is all about?"

"No clue. They just showed up at my apartment and knocked on the door. I'm an Uber driver. They started asking me questions about one of my riders from two nights ago. Something musta happened to her, but they never told me what. Other than that, like I said, I have no clue."

"Then let's get them back in here," he says, "and find out what's what. But first things first."

"What's that?"

"Would you like me to represent you?" he asks.

"Yes, sir. I mean, yes, Bernie. Definitely."

"Do you have any cash on you?" he asks.

"A few dollars."

"Give me something to make it official."

I reach into my pocket, pull out some cash. Peel off a $20, hand it to Bernie. "This enough?"

"More than enough." He takes the money with his left hand, shakes my hand with his right.

—

Bernie and I are sitting on one side of the table. His briefcase and yellow legal pad are on top of the table.

The detectives return, sit on the other side of the table.

"Let's not fuck around," Bernie says. "Pam, what's going on?"

"I'll tell you what we know, Bernie," she says. "You take it from there."

"Fair enough. Lay it on me, baby."

"Your client here is an Uber driver," she begins. "Two nights ago he picked up one Miss Rita Forsythe at the Babes in Toyland topless club on Columbus Boulevard in South Philadelphia."

"I see." The lawyer makes a note on the legal pad. "So we're talking about a stripper here."

"Always one to sugar coat," the male detective says.

Bernie ignores the remark. "Next."

"Your client," she continues, "then transported Miss Forsythe to her place of residence at the Media Station Apartments."

"Ah, Media Station." Bernie makes another note. "Lived there after I finished law school. What building?"

"The A Building," she says.

"My building." He makes anther note. "Top of the hill. Know it well." He turns his head toward me. "Do you agree with what's been said thus far?"

"Yes, Bernie."

"Next," the lawyer says to the detectives.

"Miss Forsythe," the female continues, "did not report for work the following day."

"The strip club?"

"Correct," she says. "Subsequently, two of her fellow employees went to Media Station to check on her whereabouts. But they got no response from inside her apartment. Then, with some assistance from the manager, two local officers found Miss Forsythe inside her apartment. She was dead."

"Dead?" I say.

"Just the right amount of surprise, young man," Bernie says. "Perfect reaction. Not overdone. Not underdone. Perfect." He addresses the female. "What was the cause of death?"

"Accidental drug overdose," she says, "at this point."

"Why just at this point?" Bernie asks.

"No autopsy yet to make it official."

"Way I see it," Bernie says, "you have absolutely no grounds on which to hold my client one minute longer."

"Not true," she says. "We believe Miss Forsythe obtained a quantity of illegal drugs from your client. And we believe they were the drugs that killed her."

"What evidence do you *possess*," Bernie says, "to support your wild accusations?"

"This is an open investigation," she says. "Since your client has not been charged–"

"Save the clumsy footwork, Pam," he says. "You got *nada* and you know it. Otherwise you'd already have my client in the lockup."

"We have enough to hold him," the male detective says.

"On what charges?" the lawyer asks.

"Reasonable suspicion," he says.

"Bullshit," the lawyer says. "You don't have the slightest sniff of *any* suspicion, let alone *reasonable* suspicion. So don't make me laugh." He turns his head toward me. "Young man, did you supply drugs of any kind to this stripper?"

"No way."

"Will the police find any evidence to incriminate you?"

"No way."

"Case closed." Bernie picks up his legal pad. Puts it inside his briefcase, closes the briefcase. "Now let's get the hell out of here."

"Always the jokester," the male detective says.

"Bullshit, Donald," Bernie says. "This is no joking matter. Not one judge on this planet would bind my client over for trial on such flimsy innuendo, and you know it."

CHAPTER 18

Bernie and I are walking through the main lobby inside the courthouse. One floor above where the interrogation took place. We pass through the metal detector, spin through the revolving doors, start down the marble courthouse steps.

"Don't know where to start," I say. "All I can say is thanks, Bernie. Thanks a million."

"All in a day's work," Bernie says. "Way I see it, they have no evidence. Just trying to rattle you into making some sort of confession."

"Cross my heart, Bernie, I don't have anything to confess."

"So it seems," he says without conviction.

"You believe me, don't you?"

"Never entered my mind one way or the other."

"I swear. I'm telling you the truth."

"Okay." Neither endorsement nor denial in his tone.

"Before you got here, they made it sound like they were gonna arrest me."

"Fortunately," Bernie says, "I was in my office when Mike called. Right across the street." He reaches into a jacket pocket. Produces a business card, hands it to me. "Young man, this is both hello and goodbye. Call my office at your earliest convenience and make arrangements to pay my bill."

"No problem."

"Good luck to you." He smiles. "And stay out of trouble. Nothing personal, but I don't ever want to see you again."

We reach the sidewalk. Shake hands, go our separate ways. Bernie crosses the street, keeps walking down the block.

I step up to a hot dog stand on the sidewalk.

I'm eating a soft pretzel with mustard when my Envoy pulls up. Jess behind the wheel. She sees me standing next to the cart and stops.

"Want anything?" I hold up what's left of the pretzel.

"No thanks," she says.

Put the last bite in my mouth, start chewing. Walk around to the passenger side. The pretzel's gone by the time I open the door and climb inside.

"No kiss?" she asks.

"Sorry. My mind's going around in circles." I lean across the center console, give her a quick kiss on the lips.

"You taste like mustard."

"Gee, wonder why."

"Hate to bring this up. But what the fuck's going on?" She puts the Envoy in gear, gives it a little gas.

"Where's your car?" We left her car in town last night. Drove back to my apartment in the Envoy. No clue where she parked.

"In the parking garage. Know where that is?"

"I'm an Uber driver, remember. Pretty much know where everything is these days. Make a left at the corner."

The garage is six blocks away. Because of one-way streets, we have to go all the way around the courthouse in the opposite direction. Then drive back in the right direction.

"Seriously," she says. "What's going on?"

"I'm not sure."

"What do you mean you're not sure," she says. "Never so scared in my whole life. Police knocking on your door and hauling you away."

"Technically, they didn't haul me away. They asked me to go with them and I agreed."

"From what I saw," she says, "it sure seemed like they hauled you away. And it seemed like they arrested you."

"After a while that's how it seemed to me, too."

"What did they want?" she asks.

"Said they wanted me to answer a few questions. But that was bullshit. They had some sort of hidden agenda."

"Like what?" she asks.

"Here's everything I know," I say. "Ready?"

"Been ready for the last three hours."

"On the night I met you," I start to explain, "about an hour before I picked you up, I was in South Philly, near Geno's. You know where Geno's is, right?"

"Of course."

"Got a request for a ride from a topless club."

"A strip club," she says. "Hmm, interesting. What did this stripper look like?"

"Dark hair."

"That's it?" she asks.

"And pretty."

"Getting back to my original question," she says, "what happened?"

"Nothing. Picked her up and drove her home."

"So you just picked up this stripper," she says, "and drove her home. Is that what you're trying to tell me?"

"I'm not *trying* to tell you anything. I'm *telling* you what happened. At least, that's what I thought happened. But, now, as it turns out, it's more complicated than that."

"How complicated?" she asks.

"Pretty fucking complicated. She was loaded down with a buncha things to carry."

"Like what?" she asks.

"A makeup case and two shopping bags. Anyway, she asked me to help her carry her things."

"Why?"

"Before I picked her up, she had a fight with a bouncer at the club. An old boyfriend. He twisted her wrist. It was swollen by the time we reached her building."

"So nice guy that you are," she says, "you just volunteered to help her carry her things?"

"No. I already told you. *She* asked *me* to help *her*."

"Whatever."

"Don't give me *whatever*. Don't *ever* give me whatever."

"Sorry," she says. "So, did anything happen with this stripper?"

"Like what?"

"You know exactly what I mean," she says. "Like what happened with you and me? Or like what happened with you and Margo?"

"No way."

We reach the entrance to the garage. A tri-level.

"What should I do now?" she asks.

"Pull in and drive to your car."

"If I pull in," she says, "you have to pay to get out."

"Big deal."

She pulls inside the garage. Stops, takes a slip out of the machine. "So where do the cops come into this?" She starts heading toward the ramp leading up to the next level.

"They found her dead the next day."

She hits the brakes out of reflex. The Envoy stops abruptly, the momentum carries our upper bodies forward. Her seatbelt and the steering wheel save her, but I need both hands against the dashboard to brace myself.

"Bad stop," I say.

"Sorry about that." She taps the gas and we're moving again. "What happened to her?"

"Sounds like she OD'd."

"Where do you fit into all this?" she asks.

"The cops found out she left the club in an Uber. They contacted Uber and found out I was the driver. That makes me the last person seen with her while she was still alive. That makes me the prime suspect."

"Suspect to what?" she asks.

"Selling her the drugs that killed her."

A spot's open next to her car. She pulls in, parks. Turns to face me. "Did you?"

"Can't believe you just asked me that. Do I look like a drug dealer to you?"

"People aren't always the way they seem to be," she says.

"Did I ever mention anything about drugs?"

"No."

"Did I ever give you any indication I was involved in drugs in any way, shape, or form?"

"No."

"Did you see anything drug-related in my apartment?"

"No."

"Then draw your own conclusions."

"But," she says, "you never considered any of this important enough to mention it to me?"

"There was nothing mention. Until now. She was just another ride two nights ago. I picked her and dropped her off. Then I drove to Bryn Mawr and picked you up. End of story."

"Why didn't they arrest you?" she asks.

"My Friend saved my ass."

"Your friend?"

"Not *your friend. My Friend.* That's what I call him, like it's his name. My Friend. You know, one of the guys you met last night at Pinocchio's. One of the wrestlers."

"Which one?" she asks.

"The good-looking one."

"Oh."

"I called him. Told him I was in jail and needed a lawyer. Next thing I know a lawyer shows up and straightens everything out."

"Where did he come from so fast?" she asks.

"He takes care of the legal work for the wrestlers. Lucky for me, he was in his office across the street from the courthouse when My Friend called him."

"So now what happens?" she asks.

"Nothing. It's over. As far as I'm concerned this never happened. So I'm going to New York tomorrow."

"What for?" she asks.

"The next step to getting published."

CHAPTER 19

"Make a left on 42nd," I tell My Friend.

We're on Chestnut Street in his white Kia Sorrento. It's 4:50 the next morning. Still dark. Not much traffic.

"Why not straight?" he asks.

"Chestnut's fucked up because of the 24th Street Bridge. Trust me, make the left, then a right on Market."

He makes the left onto 42nd, the right onto Market, and we're 12 blocks from the train station.

"Go all the way to Schuylkill," I tell him.

"Why?"

"I love the front of the station."

Construction began right after the Great Depression and produced a masterpiece of architectural design. A touch over 100 feet tall. Neoclassical in style with some Art Deco touches thrown in. Massive Corinthian columns stand in front, 71 feet tall, made from Alabama limestone.

Hollywood filmed a couple movies there.

"Why so early?" he asks.

"Got a reserved seat for $61. Next train's an Acela. Costs $135. This early bird just saved $74."

My Friend makes a left onto Schuylkill Avenue. We're right in front of the station.

"You want me to pull in front?" he asks. "Or go around back?"

"Front, and thanks for driving me."

"You want me to pick you up?" he asks.

"No clue when I'll be back. I'll call an Uber."

He parks in between the third and fourth columns.

I'm out the door. Dressed in black from head to toe, except for a pair of white New Balance sneakers. Carrying my laptop.

—

An hour later.

Amtrak's Northeast Regional 190 is speeding northbound. Four cars long. Crossing a bridge over the Delaware River with Trenton, New Jersey, on the other side

I'm sitting in a window seat on the left side of the car. Plenty of leg room. A fold-down tray to accommodate my laptop. Plugged into an outlet to keep the battery charged. Free Wi-Fi.

A middle-aged man sits to my right. Dressed in a suit and tie. Working on an iPad.

I'm dropping in cold on the editor-in-chief of Excalibur magazine. Rose Goldenberg. Did some research. A men's magazine with nude centerfolds, they accept unsolicited mystery stories from unpublished authors.

Hope I can convince her to look at my story.

We're a little less than an hour from New York City. Time to give my story one more read.

—

I step off the train at Penn Station.

Find myself surrounded by a sea of commuters. Busiest train station in the Western Hemisphere. Entirely underground. Under historic Madison Square Garden.

Not much better when I get out on the street. Looks even more congested. More people, plus dozens of cars, cabs, and buses.

Not 7 o'clock yet. A little better than two hours to kill. Start looking for a coffee shop. Starbucks sits on the corner to the right. No thanks. Only went to Starbucks once in my life. Once was enough.

Find a hole-in-the wall two blocks away. Called Wally's. Two people standing at a counter picking up take-out. Four small tables and chairs inside. None of the tables occupied.

I enter, step up to the counter.

"Can I help you?" the man behind the counter asks.

"I'll take a coffee please."

"For here? Or to go?"

"Here."

"You're from Philadelphia," he says. "Ain't ya?"

"Right outside the city. How'd you know?"

"Good with accents." He turns to get an empty cup. Holds it up. "This size okay?"

"Perfect."

He fills the cup. Returns a few seconds later, sets the cup on the counter. "Cream and sugar's right there. Help yourself."

"Is it all right if I linger a little?"

"Take all the time ya want, buddy. Rent's paid. Nobody'll want a table until around noon."

"Are those blueberry doughnuts back there?"

"Old fashioned blueberry *cake* doughnuts."

"I'll take one."

He turns to get a plate. Soon returns with two doughnuts.

"Second one's on me," he says.

—

I'm walking south on Sixth Avenue less than a block from Wally's. Drank a second cup of coffee before I left. Never looked at the prices, gave him a $10 when I left. Told him to keep the change, he never complained.

Enter a building a block later. Excalibur's office is on the 12th floor. Plan to get there as soon as the doors open at 9 o'clock.

A uniformed doorman is standing at a podium in the middle of the lobby, talking to a woman. A man's standing behind the woman, waiting to talk to the doorman.

I walk straight toward the elevators.

"Can I help you, sir?" the doorman calls out.

"I have a meeting with Rose Goldenberg."

"Please wait your turn, sir," he says. "I'll call her."

I keep going straight toward a bank of elevators. "I'm in a hurry. A touch late. She knows I'm coming. Been here before."

"Please wait your turn, sir."

Fortunately a bell rings as soon as I press the button. The door opens. I step onto the elevator, ride it to the 12th floor. Get off. Start walking down the hall, looking at the numbers on the doors.

Here it is. I double-check the number. Try the handle, but it doesn't turn. I knock. Wait almost a minute without a response. Knock again, louder this time.

The door finally opens.

A woman's standing there in a bathrobe and slippers, probably 40. Disheveled hair. Looks like she just crawled out of bed.

"Who the fuck are you?" she asks in a New York accent.

Not exactly the greeting I was hoping for.

She starts looking me up and down with suspicious eyes.

"I'm Steve Piasecki. I emailed you the other day about a story I'm working on."

"I don't remember," she says.

"I'm not making it up."

"Neither am I," she says. "But this is my apartment. Where I live. You can't just come in here and knock on my door."

"Sorry. This is the address on your website, so I assumed it was your office. My mistake. Didn't mean to bother you."

I turn to leave.

"Hold on," she says.

"Yeah?" I turn back to face her.

She glances at my laptop. "We don't open for business until 10. But you're here and I'm here. So, you got what you want." She steps back. "Come in."

CHAPTER 20

The autopsy of Rita Forsythe begins at 9 a.m. sharp.

Dr. Nakamura presiding. Detectives Bishop and Chase observing. A morgue attendant named Bert assisting.

Dr. Nakamura puts on a pair of rubber gloves. Turns on a voice-activated recording device.

"Body is that of well-developed, well-nourished white female. Appears to be at least 22, perhaps up to 26 years of age."

Picks up the report he made at the time of the discovery of the body, glances at it.

"Estimated time of death, approximately 12 to 18 hours prior to discovery of body. Three articles of jewelry observed on victim's body at time of discovery. Said jewelry since removed."

Passes the report to the attendant.

Measures the body. "Height: 67 inches."

Weighs the body. "Weight: 124 pounds."

Probes the head. "No signs of fracture anywhere in skull area."

Looks at the face and neck. "No visible cuts or bruises on face or neck."

Moves to the torso. "No bondage marks of any kind. No tattoos visible."

Looks at the arms. "No marks on either arm. No tattoos visible."

Pauses the recorder to address Det. Chase. "Detective, you are probably more familiar with this milieu than myself. If she's a habitual drug user, how do you explain the lack of needle marks?"

"Her body was her living," the detective replies. "She chose not to deface it. Musta snorted the shit, or smoked it, instead of shooting it."

"I will take that for what it's worth," Dr. Nakamura says. "But when using the drug in that manner, it takes a little longer to take effect. Unfortunately for the addict, the euphoria does not last as long and often leads to binges to sustain the euphoria. Which often leads to this."

Dr. Nakamura turns the recorder back on, looks at the victim's hands. "No marks on left wrist. Observe edema on right wrist indicative of grade-one sprain. Based on location and extent of swelling, edema caused by twisting of wrist."

"Signs of a struggle?" Det. Bishop wonders.

Dr. Nakamura pauses the recorder. "Possible."

"Maybe someone killed her," Det. Chase suggests. "Then tried to make it look like she OD'd."

"While such a scenario is possible," Dr. Nakamura responds, "it's extremely remote from what I have observed thus far."

"But it is a possibility," Det. Chase persists.

"If you insist," Dr. Nakamura says. "But let us keep looking."

He turns the recorder back on, inspects the genital area. "No indications of recent sexual activity. Seems to rule out any sort of sex-crime."

"I got a question," Det. Chase says.

Dr. Nakamura shuts off the recorder. "Yes, detective."

"Since her body was submerged for several hours," Det. Chase says, "wouldn't that remove any signs of sexual activity?"

"It very well could," Dr. Nakamura replies, "if the sex were consensual. However, if the sex were forceful, then some signs could still be visible. But I do not see any."

"So where do we stand?" Det. Bishop asks.

Dr. Nakamura steps away from the body. "Nothing I observed today," he begins – but stops abruptly. Begins staring at the victim's head.

"Something wrong?" Det. Bishop asks.

"Hold on," Dr. Nakamura says. "Looking from this angle, I may have missed something."

"Like what?" Det. Bishop asks.

"Hold on." Dr. Nakamura approaches the victim's head. "Let's not be premature." He leans closer. Mumbles to himself as he slowly elevates the cadaver's chin to get a better look underneath. "Right there." He points.

"Where?" Det. Bishop asks.

"Look closely." Dr. Nakamura's pointing at the throat.

Both detectives lean forward.

Dr. Nakamura turns the recorder back on. "Observe feint patterned contusions on anterior portion of neck. Both sides of larynx." Probes the area. "Possible cartilage damage."

He lifts the victim's left eyelid. "Observe slight conjunctiva in left eyeball."

Releases the left eyelid, lifts the right eyelid. "Also observe slight conjunctiva in right eyeball."

Releases the right eyelid, pauses the recorder.

"Cuff please, Bert."

The attendant moves to a row of cabinets along the near wall. Returns moments later with a blood pressure cuff.

Dr. Nakamura attaches the cuff. "Attached blood pressure cuff to upper left arm of victim."

Starts squeezing the ball to pump up the cuff. Stops to look at the dial. Gives it a few more pumps, stops again to look.

"Inflated cup high enough to constrict flow of blood, but not high enough to close the artery. Observe geographic distribution of petechiae on left forearm. Also on left hand."

Shuts off the recorder.

"What does all that mean?" Det. Bishop says.

"Possible symptoms of manual strangulation."

"Why didn't you see them before?" Det. Chase asks.

"Such symptoms," Dr. Nakamura says, "are not always apparent upon discovery of the body. And if the victim were unconscious, due to intoxication, or the ingestion of an opioid, as we believe happened in this case, not much force would be necessary to effect a lethal strangulation. Therefore, there was no superficial damage to observe at the time of discovery."

"So what changed?"

"The skin dried somewhat," Dr. Nakamura says, "and became more transparent. Which allowed the marks to become visible. Yet the marks are still so feint I almost missed them."

"Hold on a second," Det. Chase says. "Let me get this straight. Are you now saying she was strangled?"

"To be perfectly accurate, detective," Dr. Nakamura answers, "I am not saying anything. Instead, I am theorizing that the victim *might* have been strangled."

"So how do you prove it one way or the other?"

"Only one way to be certain. Time to cut. Bert."

The attendant walks over to a workstation. Attaches a new rotary blade to the autopsy saw. Returns, hands the saw to Dr. Nakamura.

Dr. Nakamura turns on the recorder, describes the procedure as he goes.

He steps up to the left side of the body. Makes a deep incision just under the left shoulder. Cuts all the way to the top of the left breast. Carefully curves around the inside of the breast. Stops cutting at the breastbone.

Moves to the right side of the body. Makes a deep incision just under the right shoulder. Cuts all the way to the top of the right breast. Carefully curves around the inside of the breast. Stops cutting at the intersection with the first cut.

"Scalpel," he says.

Bert takes the saw, hands him a scalpel.

Dr. Nakamura peels back the skin, some muscle tissue, and some soft tissue. Takes hold of the large chest flap he just created. Pulls it up, over the victim's face to expose the ribcage and throat area.

Pauses the recorder.

"Here comes the tricky part," he tells the detectives. "I must now remove the larynx, thyroid bone, and tongue. Yet keep them all conjoined as if they were a single body part."

Several minutes of careful cutting removes all three items in one piece, exposing the laryngeal skeleton. He looks at the area, probes gently.

Turns the recorder back on. "Observe several small cartilage fractures surrounding throat. Indicating cause of death to be manual strangulation." Turns off the recorder.

"So someone killed her after all," Det. Chase concludes.

"So it would seem, detective."

"So you're changing the cause of death?" Det. Bishop asks.

"The cause of death," Dr. Nakamura says, "is now homicide by means of manual strangulation."

CHAPTER 21

Early the next morning.

Despite the awkward introduction to Rose Goldenberg, my New York trip ended well. Who knew she ran the magazine out of her apartment and didn't open for business until 10.

I pled my case. She bought it, agreed to give my story a fair shake. Now I hafta back up my words.

I go online to check Excalibur's editorial requirements.

• Material never published before – check.

• No multiple submissions – check.

• Word limit 5,000 words – check.

• Must include at least two graphic sex scenes of at least 500 words each. The sex scenes must flow organically and fit seamlessly within the overall plot – Can't check this one.

My story's already 5,000 words. First, I hafta delete 1,000 words of existing plot. Next, create two graphic sex scenes of 500 words each. And finally, weave the new scenes invisibly into the story and make it shine.

Sounds like a lot of work. And it is, don't get me wrong. But believe it or not, the two graphic sex scenes will be easy to create. Thanks to an old girlfriend.

Let's call her Carolyn. Always full of surprises, she instigated at least a dozen graphic sex scenes during our time together. Only need two.

Here's one. We're driving across the Walt Whitman Bridge one night on our way home from the shore. Traffic's heavy. Cars all around us. Takes my full focus.

Suddenly she says, "What do you think, baby?"

I glance to the right, see she's balls-ass naked.

She unzips my jeans. Climbs on top of me and we're fucking. She's bouncing up and down, and screaming. I'm looking over one shoulder, then the other, trying to avoid smashing into any cars.

Scary as hell. But a whole lotta fun.

The scene needs some embellishment. Plus a couple trigger words to add sexual zing. But it's a good start.

The second scene comes after dinner one night in Olde City.

We leave the restaurant, walk a couple blocks to the car. It's parallel parked on Front Street, between Walnut and Chestnut. Almost bumper to bumper. Takes four or five back-ups and pull-forwards to work my way out. Which takes my full attention.

Once again I miss seeing her stripping down.

She unzips me. Gets on her knees on the passenger seat, starts blowing me as we pull away. Which plants her bare ass against the passenger window, giving pedestrians and passing cars an interesting sideshow.

Again, the scene needs some embellishment and a few trigger words. But these two scenes will come across realistic as hell because they really happened.

I'm ready to get started, but someone's knocking on the door.

Jess. Perfect timing. Sexual memories are flowing. With barely a hello, I lead her into the bedroom.

—

An hour later.

"Want to do it again?" she asks.

"Again?" I pretend to whine.

Jess rolls toward me. Leans over, kisses my cheek. "Well?" she pushes.

"You must think I'm some sort of sex machine."

"You do have some skills in that department," she says. "You definitely know your way around, shall we say, this and that."

"Police! Open up!" Suddenly comes from the front door. A loud knocking follows, and another shout. "Police! Open up!"

"Not again," she says.

"What the fuck?" I bolt out of bed naked. "Be right there!"

I put on my jeans and sneakers. No time for socks.

"What should I do?" she asks.

"Get dressed. Oh, and call my lawyer. His card's on the bureau."

Next comes my black shirt from yesterday, buttoning it while walking down the hall.

Open the door, see the same two detectives standing outside. Behind them, a uniformed police officer and two men in coveralls.

"What the fuck?" I say.

"Search warrant," the female detective says.

The male detective sticks the warrant in my face. "You have the right to remain silent. But anything you say, can, and will be used against you in a court of law. You have the right to an attorney. If you cannot afford one at this time, one will be appointed to you by the court. With these rights in mind, are you willing to talk with us?"

"Just one word."

"What's that?" the detective says.

"Go fuck yourself."

"That's three words," he replies.

"No shit, Sherlock."

The police officer spins me around, handcuffs me. Leads me out of my apartment, down the stairs, outside to a police car parked at the curb.

CHAPTER 22

The detectives start searching the apartment.

Det. Bishop opens the top drawer of one of the file cabinets. Starts leafing through the file folders.

Det. Chase starts looking at the books in the bookcase. "This guy's obsessed with crime. That's all he reads about."

"Writes about it, too." She pulls a small box out of the bottom drawer. "This is computer software for writers."

"Big deal," Det. Chase says. "Way I see it, the more he reads, the more he learns. And the more he writes, the more he gets curious about getting away with murder."

"Just like Leopold and Loeb."

"Who?"

"Two college kids," she says. "Rich Jew boys from Chicago back in the 1920s. Genius IQs. Thought they could commit a perfect murder and get away with it. Several books about them, including Compulsion."

"Ding-ding-ding." Det. Chase pulls Compulsion out of the bookcase. "Here it is."

"No shit."

"Looks like this guy decided to act one out."

"You really think he killed her?"

"Who else?" he replies.

One of the men in coveralls walks up.

"What do you want us to take?" he asks.

"Let's see." Det. Bishop looks around the room. "Laptop, printer, all the books. And wheel out the file cabinets."

—

The arresting officer leads me through a small cellblock. Brighter than I imagined. Only two cells, both empty.

He stops right there. Removes the handcuff from my left wrist. "Put your left hand on the wall. Up high."

I reach up, place my left hand on the wall.

He removes the handcuff from my right wrist. "Put your right hand on the wall. Up high."

I reach up, place my right hand on the wall. Stand silently while he pats me down.

He points to the right. "We're going through that door."

A few steps later we're in a large lobby.

"Stop at the counter up there," he says.

I stop at the counter. A sheet of bullet-proof glass separates me from a middle-aged woman on the other side.

"Do you have any identification, sir?" she asks.

"Front pocket." I nod downward. "May I?"

"Yes, you may, sir."

I reach into my pocket, pull out some folded money. Find my driver's license in between the money.

An aluminum basket slides out from underneath the counter.

"Please place your ID inside the basket, sir."

I place my license inside the basket, then the basket slides back underneath the counter.

She looks at my license. "Steven Piasecki?"

"Yep."

She confirms my address, height, weight, and social security number while simultaneously keypunching the information into a computer. She sends the basket back out. "There's your driver's license, Mr. Piasecki."

"Thank you." I pick it up, put it back inside my pocket.

"Mr. Piasecki," she says, "you are being charged with possession of a controlled substance, possession of said controlled substance with intent to distribute, and the sale of said controlled substance. Do you understand those charges against you?"

"Ma'am, if I may be so bold, I have no clue why I'm being charged with anything."

"I understand," she replies without meaning it. "Would you like to contact a lawyer?"

"Already in progress."

"Good." She continues with the script. "Mr. Piasecki, are you now, or have you ever been, a member of any gang or drug cartel?"

"You're kidding, right?" I laugh for effect.

"No, sir," she says. "I am quite serious."

"Do I look like a member of a gang or a drug cartel?"

"In my opinion, Mr. Piasecki, you do not. But looks are sometimes deceiving."

"Not in my case."

"I understand. Please remove your personal belongings and deposit them inside the receptacle."

The officer's now holding a plastic container. One like you might use to store clothing or dirty laundry.

"Like what?" I ask.

"Your keys. Watch, rings, jewelry, wallet, phone. And your belt."

I have 32 dollars in cash, my license, a debit card, and cellphone. I deposit everything inside the container.

"Mr. Piasecki," she says, "you may keep your socks on–"

"Didn't have time to put my socks on."

"In that case," she says, "you may keep your shoes on if you remove the laces."

"Not planning on hanging myself."

"I am sure you are not," she says.

I bend down, remove my shoelaces. Stand up, place the laces inside the plastic container.

"Thank you," she says. "Is that everything?"

"Yep."

The officer takes over. "No keys?"

"Left them in my apartment."

"Watch?"

"Don't own one."

"Wallet?"

"Don't own one."

"Belt?"

"Never wear one."

The officer leads me back the way we came in.

We reach the spot where he patted me down.

"Stop."

I stop.

"Just a warning for your own good," he says. "From this point on, if I find any weapons or contraband on your person, you'll be charged with a felony. Do you understand?"

"Got neither."

"Strip down."

Uh-oh. Never saw this coming.

Takes me a minute to get down to just my shoes. No two ways about it, this is the most embarrassing moment in my life.

"This will go a lot easier," he says, "if you put your hands against the wall. Just like last time."

I assume the position. My back facing him, both hands high up on the wall. Takes a few seconds.

"Turn around," he says.

I turn around.

His eyes scan me up and down. "Put your clothes back on."

Thank God. No cavity search. I dress fast.

"Now what?"

"Take your pick." He points at the empty cells.

I pick the one on the right. Step inside, hear the cell door slam shut behind me.

—

Seated around a table are the chief of C.I.D., the DA, his chief prosecutor, detectives Bishop and Chase, and Dr. Nakamura.

"A little while ago," the chief begins, "Pam and Donald arrested the Uber driver. He's charged with possession, intent to distribute, and sales. Booked and processed. He'll be arraigned in district court this afternoon."

"But," the DA interjects, "as we all know by now, when Ken performed the autopsy this morning, he found evidence of manual strangulation. And he changed the cause of death to homicide."

"So," the chief interjects, "we now believe this Uber driver used the drugs to disguise the fact he strangled her."

"But," the DA says, "the change to homicide is problematic. We don't have enough evidence to arrest him on the homicide charge. So if any one of you is called as a witness, it's extremely critical that you don't mention anything about it."

"What if his attorney brings up the autopsy?" Dr. Nakamura asks.

"To begin with," the prosecutor says, "he doesn't know about the autopsy. But if it somehow comes up, I'll object and sweep it under the rug. Just don't you mention it."

"So you want me to perjure myself?" Dr. Nakamura asks.

"Just pretend the cause of death remains accidental overdose. Nobody outside this room knows about the autopsy."

"Not quite," Dr. Nakamura says.

"Who else knows?" the prosecutor asks.

"My assistant was present."

CHAPTER 23

The police car pulls into a parking spot in front of the district court. I see Bernie, briefcase in hand, waiting for me.

The officer helps me out of the car.

"Didn't think I'd ever see you again," Bernie says. "Certainly not this soon, anyway."

"Makes us even."

—

Two minutes later.

Bernie's sitting on one side of a small table. His briefcase and a yellow legal pad sit on top of the table.

I'm sitting on the other side. "Now what?"

"You're charged with a series of drug offenses."

"That's what I heard, Bernie, but that's bullshit."

"That may be," he says. "But I've done a little research since your girlfriend called me. Two C.I.D. detectives and a pair of evidence techs searched your apartment a little while ago."

"I was there when they showed up. What the hell they looking for?"

"Your stash," he says.

"What stash?"

"The drugs that killed the stripper," he says.

"More bullshit, Bernie. There's no stash."

"Do you have any scales in your apartment?"

"I don't even have a bathroom scale."

"What about a large supply of plastic baggies?"

"None. I don't cook."

"Large quantity of money?" he asks.

"I keep loose change in a Styrofoam cup in the kitchen. Only way they find any stash is if they plant it there."

"Hope you're right," he says.

"You don't believe me?"

"Young man," he says, "here are the facts of life when it comes to our legal system. Neither guilt nor innocence matter to the prosecutor or myself. He's going to try to get a conviction and I'm going to try to get an acquittal. All that matters is winning or losing and, trust me, we're both going to bust our balls trying to win."

"So where do we go from here?"

"We start with a few questions." He looks at a checklist on his legal pad. "Do you have a prior criminal record?"

"Not even a parking ticket."

"Are you perceived to be a threat to a family member, spouse, former spouse, or any member of the public-at-large?"

"Not sure what you mean."

"A restraining order?"

"No."

"How long have you lived at your current address?" he asks.

"Going on three years."

"Before that?" he asks.

"Lived in Delco all my life."

"Your last name? Are you related to Piasecki Helicopters?"

"Frank Piasecki was my great-grandfather."

"Wonderful." He makes a note. "Any record of drug or alcohol abuse?"

"No."

"DUI?"

"No."

"Ever attempt suicide, or threaten to commit suicide?"

"No way."

"Weapons offenses?"

"None."

"Good answers," he says. "Now, using all of the wisdom at my disposal, we're looking at one of three things. One, they found some sort of *prima facie* evidence to connect you to the drugs."

"Like what?"

"Maybe they found your fingerprints in the bathroom," he says. "Like on the drug baggie, the mirror, or on the vanity."

"Impossible. Never touched any drug baggies in my whole life. Never set one foot inside her apartment."

"A witness perhaps," he suggests.

"To what? I didn't do anything."

"Let's move on to supposition number two," he says. "They hope to push you to the point where you rat out the prime players in your drug cartel."

"That's crazy. I'm not part of any drug cartel."

"Which leaves us with my third scenario."

"Which is?"

"They're after something bigger," he says.

"Like what?"

"This is way out there," he says. "But what if she didn't die from a drug overdose? What if someone killed her and then tried to cover it up by making it look like an overdose?"

"That someone being me?"

"Precisely," he says.

"That's preposterous."

"Just thinking out loud," he says. "Just trying to predict every possibility we *may* encounter. We'll start getting answers once your arraignment gets started." Bernie stares straight into my eyes. "Did you supply her with any drugs?"

"Cross my heart, Bernie. I never gave her any drugs. Picked her up and drove her home. And then I carried her belongings up to her apartment and left."

"What?" he says. "Hold on. You carried her belongings into her apartment? You just said you never set one foot inside her apartment."

"I carried her belongings *up to* her apartment. Not *into* it. I set everything on the floor *outside* her apartment. Never went inside."

"Why did you carry her things?"

"She told me she had an argument with one of the bouncers, you know, before she left the club. An old boyfriend. He twisted her wrist. It was swollen by the time we reached her building and she asked me to help carry her things."

"What did you carry?" he asks.

"A makeup case, a heavy one, and two shopping bags. From Macy's, I think. And, oh, yeah, a riding crop fell out of one of the shopping bags. She picked it up and handed it to me. Then I put it back inside one of the bags."

"A riding crop." Bernie chuckles. "Brings back memories. That riding crop may be where they found your fingerprint. Remote at best, but possible. Plus, your prints could be on that makeup case or the shopping bags."

"Guess you're right."

"So you helped her," Bernie says, "and wound up getting yourself in a whole shitload of trouble. Who'd a thunk it?"

Bitter irony flashes into my brain. My Friend told me that helping people was gonna get me in trouble one day. I thought he was so fulla shit, but somehow he nailed it.

"So that's it?" Bernie snaps me back to the here and now. "Or is there anything else to consider?"

"Not that I can think of."

"Good," he says. "Oh, almost forgot. You mentioned something about an argument with one of the bouncers. Did she mention his name?"

"Sal."

"Good," he says. "Maybe we can throw him into the mix in your defense. Now, when the judge asks you to enter a plea, what do you say?"

"Not guilty."

"Correct," he says. "The Eighth Amendment guarantees you the right to post bond while you await trial. So the judge will set bail. Based on the particulars in this case, your bail should be somewhere around, say, $10,000."

"Ten grand? What the fuck?"

"Relax," he says. "I've been working with the same bail bondsman for years. He'll post bond for you. For a small fee."

"How small?"

"As a special favor to me," he says, "he'll charge you $100. Not exactly get out of jail free, but pretty goddam close."

"Thanks, Bernie."

"Oh, almost forgot."

"What?"

"Can you in any way," he asks, "document the time after you left the stripper's apartment?"

"Got a request for another ride as I was pulling away from her building."

"And you took that ride?" he verifies.

"Yep."

"Why didn't you mention that before?" he says. "That could be the key to saving your ass."

Suddenly there's a knock on the door.

"Come in," Bernie calls out.

The door opens. "The judge is ready for you."

CHAPTER 24

Bernie and I are standing outside the door to the courtroom.

"Show time." He opens the door, we enter. A wide aisle runs down the middle with rows of chairs on both sides, but no one's there. Arraignments are closed to the public.

A female judge is sitting behind the bench. Wearing a black robe and glasses. I'm guessing early 50s.

The bailiff looks around, sees us. Calls our case.

We start down the aisle, reach a railing and stop.

"Good afternoon, your honor," Bernie greets the judge.

"Good afternoon to you, Mr. Wald."

Bernie swings open a double-gate, directs me to a table on the left. I move behind the table. Bernie stops next to me, places his briefcase on the table.

"Sit down," he instructs me.

We both sit in the chairs behind the table.

I hear a commotion behind us. Turn my head, catch a glimpse of a well-dressed man carrying a briefcase.

"Mr. Baldino," the judge says. "I feel somewhat honored to have the district attorney's chief prosecutor in my humble court today."

"Thank you, your honor," he says. "Nice to see you as well."

The prosecutor passes through the gates. Steps over to a table on the right, remains standing. Sets his briefcase on the table. Opens it, begins pulling out legal-looking documents.

"Will counsel please identify themselves," the judge begins.

"Henry Baldino, your honor, assistant to the district attorney, County of Delaware, Commonwealth of Pennsylvania."

"Thank you, Mr. Baldino," the judge says.

Bernie stands, whispers, "Stand up."

I stand.

"Bernard Wald, your honor," Bernie begins, "of Wald, Reilly, and Rosenbaum. Representing Mr. Steven Piasecki for his arraignment today. Mr. Piasecki is standing to my left."

The judge reads the charges. "Mr. Piasecki, do you waive further reading of the complaint and a complete statement of your rights?"

"Say 'I do,'" Bernie whispers.

"I do."

"Do you wish to enter a plea at this time?"

"Not guilty."

"So noted." The judge makes a note.

The prosecutor lays out the facts in his case. The judge binds me over for a preliminary hearing. The whole thing takes less than 10 minutes.

Bernie stands. Places his left hand on my right shoulder, stares straight ahead at the judge.

"Your honor," he begins, "the reputation of a law-abiding citizen, without one blemish on his record, has been impugned today, with no basis in fact. Now, in regard to my client's bail– "

"Your honor," the prosecutor stands, "the Commonwealth asks that bail be denied."

"With all due respect to my esteemed colleague," Bernie says, "there are no grounds for such a request. Mr. Piasecki is a man with deep roots in the community. He spent his entire life in Delaware County. He's the great-grandson of Frank Piasecki. Mr. Frank Piasecki is the man who founded the Piasecki Helicopter Company nearly 80 years ago, right here in Delaware County. His company became Boeing Aircraft, and Boeing employs more local residents than any other commercial venture in Delaware County. Your honor, my client represents absolutely no risk of flight. I thus beseech the court to allow my client to post bail."

"Mr. Baldino," the judge says, "it does not appear to the court that Mr. Piasecki represents any sort of flight risk. Thus, I must sustain Mr. Wald's contention to deny your request."

"I understand, your honor," the prosecutor says. "But the charges in this case are serious. We are currently dealing with an opioid epidemic in this country. And as we just learned, with this case, this epidemic has now invaded our own back yard. Therefore, the Commonwealth requests that the defendant's bail reflect the severity of the charges filed against him. The Commonwealth recommends that the defendant's bail be set at no less than $100,000. Full cash."

The judge examines some paperwork.

"I'm looking at the police report for Mr. Piasecki," she says. "Other than the charges in this case, which were filed not more than four hours ago, all I see is a blank sheet of paper. Mr. Piasecki has no prior criminal history. So, Mr. Baldino, I believe $25,000 is more appropriate."

"With all due respect, your honor," Bernie says, "that amount still seems somewhat excessive. Mr. Piasecki is a working man, from an upstanding family, with the deepest of roots in our community."

The judge looks at the paperwork again. Eventually looks up. "Upon further review, the bail for Mr. Piasecki is set at $5,000."

"Thank you, your honor," Bernie says.

"Furthermore," she says, "based on Mr. Piasecki's roots in our community, I am willing to allow him to sign a signature bond holding him personally culpable for that amount."

"Thank you, your honor," Bernie says.

"Objection, your honor," the prosecutor shouts.

"Overruled," the judge says.

"But, your honor–" the prosecutor tries to object once again.

"Save it, Mr. Baldino," the judge cuts him off. "When I said 'overruled,' that's exactly what I meant. Mr. Piasecki will remain free on a personal recognizance bond until his preliminary hearing. Whether you agree with my ruling or not is irrelevant. Now do you understand, Mr. Baldino?"

"Yes, your honor," the prosecutor says.

The judge raps her gavel to end my arraignment.

—

I'm feeling pretty good as we exit the courtroom.

"Bernie, if it weren't for you, I wouldn't be walking around free as a bird right now. And without having to post bond. Thanks."

"You're welcome, young man," he says. "But how long you remain free as a bird, as you put it, is yet to be determined. Today, we just postponed the showdown. The next hurdle comes at your preliminary hearing."

"When's that?"

"By pulling a few more strings, I can get it scheduled for Friday. But it's pretty much a rubber stamp, just like today. The prosecutor reads the charges, presents a modicum of evidence, and the judge binds you over for a formal trial. That's how it goes 99 times out of 100."

"And then comes a trial?"

"Correct," he says. "In the courthouse. In Media. In front of a real judge. And a jury of your peers."

"But, Bernie, there's no evidence against me."

"I hate to say it, young man," he says, "but they must have *something*. Otherwise we wouldn't be this far along."

"What do I do in the meantime?"

"Don't do anything stupid," he says. "Relax. Let the cards play out. Hibernate."

"No problem. Got plenty to keep me busy."

"Good," he says. "Do you need a ride?"

A horn beeps as my silver Envoy comes into view. Jess behind the wheel. She pulls up, stops. Lowers the driver's window, smiles.

"And who do we have here?" Bernie asks.

"I'm his girlfriend." Jess gives him a big smile.

"Is that right?" Bernie says.

Jess nods, keeps smiling.

"This is my crackerjack attorney," I say. "Bernie Wald."

"A pleasure to meet you, Mr. Wald."

"Just call me Bernie," he says.

"Pleased to meet you, Bernie."

"We spoke on the phone," he says. "Correct?"

"Correct."

"Bernie," I interrupt, "remember when you asked if I could document the time after I left the stripper's apartment?"

"Of course."

"Meet my documentation."

"Honestly?" Bernie says with a tone of surprise.

"Yep. Meet Miss Jessika Kazlo."

"But you can call me Jess." She smiles.

"In that case, Jess," Bernie says, "it's a good idea for us to get together as soon as possible. I need a deposition from you. Is it at all possible for you to see me in my office later today. At say," looks at his watch. "six o'clock?"

"Anything to help Steve."

CHAPTER 25

"Wanta drive?" Jess asks.

"Hafta pick up my stuff at the police station. Be easier if you drive."

"Sorry I was late." She starts driving.

"You got here just in time."

"Changing the subject," she says. "My old manager just started a new gig. His name's Artie, and he wants to hire me. That's what took so long."

"Where?"

"Brand new franchise," she says. "Opening up not far from The Grog. So, what do you think I should do?"

"What do *you* think you should do?"

"Not sure," she says. "That's why I'm asking you."

"You didn't tell me anything about it."

"They're from Louisiana," she says. "An upscale operation. Sort of like Friday's, or Chickie's and Pete's, but Cajun. Won't be ready for another two months, but he'll hire me now. Lots of work to do, and he knows I'm a good worker."

"Did you enjoy working for him?"

"I did," she says. "He's a great boss."

"Sounds like you just made your own decision."

—

Doesn't take long to reach the police station.

"Drop me at the door," I say. "Shouldn't take long."

I'm out the door of the Envoy, heading for the entrance.

Five minutes later I'm exiting with all my personal belongings back in my possession.

Jess pulls up. Opens the door, gets out. "You drive."

I get behind the wheel. Wait for her to get in, then pull away.

The police station's six blocks from my apartment.

"When I ran over to Bryn Mawr," she says, "I passed a house that's for rent."

"That's nice."

"I thought *we* could take a look at it," she says.

I see an open spot right in front of my building.

"Jess, I told you. Getting established as a writer comes before anything else. Until then, I can't consider any sort of commitment."

I pull in and park.

"I have this wild idea," she says, "that, by now, we're at least boyfriend and girlfriend."

"What's your hurry to put a label on things?"

"Bottom line," she says. "I want to settle down and get married someday. Getting a place together would give us a chance to see if we're compatible.

"Jess, we just met six days ago."

"Exactly 135 hours ago," she says.

"Do you have an app keeping track of the time?"

"Speaking about time." Her tone just changed. "Let me know when you have a little time for me."

She starts getting out of the Envoy.

"Where you going?"

"Away from you," she says. "I don't want to *intrude* on your precious writing time. Give me a call when you can squeeze me in."

"Jess, wait."

She turns to face me. "What?"

"Can we at least go inside and talk about this."

She smiles.

We get out of the Envoy. I lead the way to the entrance. Unlock the door, hold it open. Jess enters in front of me. We take three steps inside the lobby.

Here comes the apartment manager running down the stairs. Steps in front of us, blocks our progress.

His name's Errol. Closing in on 60, he speaks with a slight British accent. Not very handy but likes to wear coveralls to make it look like he is. Huffing and puffing from running down the steps.

"What are you?" he asks. "A drug dealer?"

"What're you talking about?"

"Cops searched your apartment today."

"I know."

"This is a respectable place," he says.

"It's over and done with. They're gone."

"No they're not," he says.

"What're you talking about?"

"They're still here," he says.

"Where?"

He retreats to the back wall. Loops around to avoid the wall of windows facing the street. Stops behind a giant potted plant. "Come here. See for yourself."

I start moving straight toward him.

"Stop," he says. "Stay away from the windows. You want them to see you? Don't you know anything?"

"Thought I did." I back away from the windows. Loop around, wind up behind the same potted plant.

Errol points out the windows. "Right there."

I look out the windows. Takes a few seconds to see what he's talking about.

A train station sits on the other side of the street. Dozens of cars parked in the lot. One car eventually sticks out like your proverbial sore thumb.

I see two faces inside the vehicle. Both white males. One's sitting behind the wheel drinking coffee. The other's looking through a pair of binoculars.

The unmarked car's in perfect position to keep an eye on my vehicle, on the entrance to my building, and on my apartment windows three floors directly above.

Never saw either face before.

Another unmarked car pulls up. Stops beside the first car. I see both faces inside the second vehicle. The two detectives who arrested me.

"I don't know what to say," I tell Errol. "Sorry."

"Sorry don't cut it, buddy," he says. "We can't have drug deals going on here."

"I lived here for almost three years and never caused one ounce of trouble."

"Until today," he says.

"Mistaken identity, pure and simple. But thanks for letting me know about the cops."

"Make sure nothing else happens," he says. "Or else."

"Or else what?"

"Or else I revoke your lease and kick you the hell out."

"Just try it. My brother's a lawyer. He'll sue the living shit out of you. I'll wind up owning this building and kick *your ass* the hell out."

—

Jess and I climb the two flights to reach my floor. The door to my apartment's right there. We stop while I dig out the keys.

"So your brother's a lawyer," Jess says

"I don't have any brothers."

"What about sisters?"

"Nope. Only child."

"Explains a lot," she says. "So you just lied to that man?"

"Not really."

"What would you call it?" she asks.

"Exercising discretion."

"Would you ever lie to me?" she asks.

"Do you really want me to answer that?"

"I certainly do," she says.

"Only if the situation dictates."

"So you're willing to bend your rules," she says, "when it works to your advantage."

"Let me know when you're finished with the ear job."

I unlock the door, push it open for Jess.

"I'm done," she says, "for now." She enters. "Wonder if the cops took anything."

I close the door, lock it. Enter the living room, see the screensaver floating around on the TV screen. Pick up the remote. Click twice and an episode of Breaking Bad replaces the screensaver.

"Looks like all your furniture's here," she says.

"But the laptop's gone. My printer, file cabinets, and all my books." I walk over to the front windows, peer outside. "Can you believe those fuckers put a tail on me?"

"Could you actually go to jail?"

"Possible, and the thought of going to jail scares the living shit out of me. But I'm not *that* worried. All they have is circumstantial innuendo to a crime I never committed. Everything will work out. So you wanta go with me?"

"Where?" she asks.

"I need a computer to revise my story."

"Aren't your files on your old laptop?"

"Yes, and no."

"How's that?" she asks.

"Every six hours I send an email to myself with the files attached. So I can get on any computer, go into my email account, and download the attachments."

"That's pretty smart," she says.

"Comes from being an only child." I start down the hallway. "Be right back."

"Where you going?" she asks.

"Gotta brush my teeth."

"You know," she says, "you have a bad attitude about our relationship."

I start brushing, pretend I can't hear her.

"You're ignoring the possibility of building a lasting relationship."

Not the only thing I'm ignoring.

"And," she says, "that's exactly what could jeopardize our relationship. Middle ground exists, you know, where we can accomplish both goals. You can work on getting published, and we can grow our relationship at the same time."

I'm gargling.

"Well?" she says.

I'm wiping my mouth with a towel when she comes walking down the hallway. "Did you say something?"

"Nothing important," she says.

"So you wanta go with me?"

"I have no desire to walk around," she says, "and watch you look for a new computer. Besides, I have to see Bernie at six."

"Oh, yeah. Right." I walk to the window, peer outside again. Only the first car there now. "But let me go first."

"Why?"

"The cops saw you come in with me, but they don't know what kind of car you drive. If I go first, they can't tail you."

"You really think they'd do that," she says.

"Bernie said they're willing to do anything. Oh, and next time you come over, park around back so they don't see you come in."

"If there is a next time."

CHAPTER 26

Jess's black Acura pulls into a parking spot in front of the Radcliff House. Picture any three-story garden complex in a tree-lined suburban community and you're looking at Radcliff House.

Jess heads straight toward the entrance.

Inside the lobby, she punches a button, waits for a response.

Half a minute passes.

"Who is it?" Margo's voice comes out of the intercom.

"Me."

"What the fuck do you want?" Margo asks.

"Something happened. Please let me in."

———

Margo's wearing a white tank top and pink bikinis as she opens the door.

"Talk fast," Margo says, "or I slam the door in your face."

"The cops arrested Steve."

"Come in," Margo says. "Don't need a scene like last time." Margo pivots and retreats into the living room.

Jess follows.

Gray sectional sofas are arranged in a U-pattern with a glass coffee table in the middle. The coffee table sits on top of a blue and burgundy Oriental throw rug. Two stainless-steel lamps and two potted palms provide accent.

Jess and Margo remain standing.

Jess says, "I was in bed with Steve this morning."

"So you came here to brag," Margo says.

"No. That's when the cops knocked on his door and arrested him."

"Back up a little," Margo says. "Start with spending the night with him."

"Spent the last *two* nights with him. Same thing happened yesterday."

"What's it all about?" Margo asks.

"Long story."

"Coffee?" Margo asks.

"Coffee's the last thing I need."

"Follow me," Margo says. "Got just what the doctor ordered." She leads Jess straight to her wine rack. Picks out a bottle, uses her best French accent, "*Chateau La Prade Côtes de Francs.*"

"You and your French."

"Sorry," Margo says, "about saying you went to a stupid fucking art school."

"Forgiven."

Margo corkscrews the bottle.

Jess locates two wine glasses, sets them on the counter.

Margo fills both glasses.

Jess lifts her glass, sniffs the bouquet.

"Well?" Margo asks.

"Plum?"

"Sharp smeller," Margo says. "Plum, along with a few other fruits beside grapes."

They tap glasses, sip the wine.

"Now let's get down to business." Margo leads Jess into the living room. Sits on one of the sectionals.

Jess sits across from her.

"On the night I met him," Jess begins, "right before he picked me up, he picked up a stripper."

"When you say picked up?" Margo says.

"With Uber. Driving. He picked her up at a strip club on Columbus Boulevard and drove her home."

"Okay," Margo says. "Keep going."

"Next day, they find the stripper dead."

"What the fuck?" Margo says. "Did he kill her?"

"God no. She OD'd. But he's the last person seen with her, so they think he supplied the drugs that killed her."

"So he's a drug dealer," Margo says.

"God, no. They questioned him and released him. That time."

"What were you doing while that was going on?"

"Hiding in the closet the first time."

"What about the second time?" Margo asks.

"Hid in the closet again today. But then I heard them start searching his apartment. Didn't want them to find me hiding in the closet. Might look suspicious, like I was guilty of something. So I got dressed and left."

"They didn't stop you?" Margo asks.

"Slipped out while they were looking the other way."

"So he's in jail now?" Margo asks.

"Out on bail. Picked him up after his arraignment and drove him home. But then all we did was bitch at each other."

"About what?" Margo asks.

"This, that, the other. And in the middle of all this, Artie called and offered me a job at a new place opening up across the street from Kelly's."

"Saw the construction," Margo says, "Looks nice. So what were you two bitching about?"

"I saw this house in Drexel Hill. A rental. You know, when I ran over to see Artie. And I liked it. So I wanted Steve to take a ride with me to take a look at it."

"You wanted Steve to look at a house with you?" Margo says. "A man you've known for less than a week?"

Jess takes out her phone and makes a few clicks. "Actually 137 hours."

"Do you have an app keeping track?"

"Sort of."

"Goddam," Margo says. "A whole 137 hours and you expect him to commit."

"You're not funny."

"Not trying to be funny," Margo says. "But you have to give a man at least 150 hours to commit. Everybody knows that."

"Still not funny."

Margo looks Jess dead in the eye. "Don't take this wrong. You're my best friend and I love you like a sister."

"But?"

"But he fucked you one night," Margo says. "He fucked me the next night. And now he's back to fucking you again. Is he really the kind of man you want to spend the rest of your life with?"

———

Bernie's office is right across the street from the courthouse.

Jess arrives for her appointment five minutes early. Enters the building. It's after hours, so the lobby's empty.

"Jess," Bernie's voice calls out. "Thank you for being punctual."

Jess walks down the corridor.

"In case I forget," she says, "thanks for all you're doing to help Steve."

"I just hope we can mitigate his situation." He takes Jess by the elbow, leads her to his office. Then to a chair in front of a huge desk. "Make yourself comfortable.

Jess takes a seat.

Bernie circles the desk, sits.

"You just made it sound," she says, "like it looks bad for him"

"This case is confusing. While it seems like no evidence, and no witnesses exist, to any wrongdoing, the prosecution is proceeding. So your testimony could be very important."

"So I'm going to be a witness?" Jess asks.

"All depends on what you tell me right now. So, with your permission, I'm going to record our conversation."

"That's why I'm here," she says.

Bernie presses a button, starts recording.

"So," he begins, "according to Steve, he picked up a rider at a topless club on Columbus Boulevard and transported her to her residence in Media. He then claims he picked you up for his next ride."

"That's right."

"Had you two ever met before?"

"No."

"But you have since consummated a relationship. Is that correct?"

"Yes."

"Pretty fast work, from complete strangers to boyfriend and girlfriend, in the blink of an eye."

"What can I say?" she says. "Love at first sight, for me. I offered to buy him a drink. We stopped, had that drink and, and we, and we had sex that first night."

"Where did these drinks take place?"

"At the Black Horse Tavern outside Phoenixville."

"Is there anyone who can verify that?"

"We both spoke with the bartender," she says. "In fact, we introduced ourselves that night. So he should remember."

CHAPTER 27

I'm carrying a box under my arm as I approach the door to my apartment. It contains my new $600 laptop.

I drove to the Concord Mall in Delaware, just above Wilmington. The trip took 40 minutes each way. I saved $36 in sales tax. Now I'm wondering if $36 is worth the extra time and travel.

I unlock the door, start to step inside.

"Hold the door," comes a voice behind me. My Friend. Called him on the way back, brought him up to speed about getting arrested.

I leave the door open, go inside. An episode of Dexter's playing.

"Place sure looks different," My Friend says. "But at least they left a place for me to sit." He sits on the couch.

I walk over to the window, peak outside. "Where'd you park?"

"Around back," he says.

"Good."

"Why?"

"An unmarked car's across the street with two undercover cops."

"You're shitting me?" he says.

"Followed me all the way to Delaware and back."

"No shit," he says.

"Wonder if they're allowed to tail me across state lines."

"You shoulda taken a picture," he says

"Took a bunch, and made sure landmarks were visible in the background." I set the box on my desk, sit in the executive chair. "Gotta unpack this computer, set it up, and get down to business. If you want anything, you know where it is."

"What do you have to do?" he asks.

"Rewrite the last story that got rejected."

"What's the story about?" he asks.

"This guy finds out his wife's been cheating. He confronts the dude, then kills him."

"How?"

"Poisons him."

"That's a little different," he says. "Not what I expected."

"That's what makes it good."

"So," he says, "it's, like, a detective story."

"Not exactly. Just those two guys, no cops. So it's a mystery."

"Interesting," he says. "You hungry?"

"Didn't eat all day because of the cop bullshit."

"Pizza?" he asks.

"No." I hand him a menu. "Find something you like."

—

It takes a lotta cursing to get my new laptop unpacked, up and running. Start editing my story.

The door opens and My Friend returns with our takeout from Big Daddyz in Folsom. He sets the bag on the coffee table. Opens it, and delightful aromas fill the room.

My Friend got a chicken breast sandwich and fries. I got a smoked kielbasa sandwich and a side of fried perogies.

I stop working. Open my perogies, but my cellphone rings. It's Jess.

"Hey," I answer. "How'd it go with Bernie?" I listen for a good minute. "That's too bad. Look, My Friend and I just got some takeout. Why don't you come over."

Says she'll be over in 15 minutes.

I spoon a little sour cream onto one of the perogies. Fork one up. Take a bite, start chewing.

"What are they?" My Friend asks.

"Perogies. Good Polish food. I grew up with them. Sorta like your ravioli, but no tomato sauce. You can put different stuff inside. These are filled with potato."

"Can I try one?" he asks.

"Yeah, but just one. Gotta save a couple for Jess." Then I lean back, start staring at the wall.

"Something wrong?" he asks.

"Jess just met with Bernie. We thought she'd be my alibi. But since I spent half an hour driving the stripper home, and dropping her off, that gave me plenty of time to sell her the drugs that killed her. Jess is after-the-fact. No help."

"Could you actually go to jail?"

"Bernie thinks they must have something that points to my guilt."

"Like what?"

"Fuck if I know. But there's gotta be something that proves I'm innocent."

CHAPTER 28

Time will be both my enemy and my ally for the next 60 hours.

My preliminary hearing begins on Friday morning. That's my enemy. But those same 60 hours give me time to rewrite my story, make it worthy of publication. That's my ally.

These 60 hours will come down to a whirlwind of writing with crime series playing in the background, camaraderie, food, and sex.

Not in any particular order.

—

I finish my kielbasa sandwich. Wipe my hands with a paper napkin, start opening my email .

My Friend and Jess are sitting on the sofa, eating. I saved half my sandwich and two perogies for her. They're getting to know each other, watching an episode of Jack Ryan.

Beautiful. Here's an email from Rose Goldenberg. Says she's pleased to meet me, follow the guidelines, and good luck.

Plenty of juggling and blending to do. Guarding against continuity errors. Balancing the theme so it's inconspicuous in the background.

A lotta cutting and pasting. Writing and editing. Rewriting and more editing .

All that said, gotta be finished by midnight on Thursday. My preliminary hearing's scheduled for 9 o'clock Friday morning. Gives me the rest of tonight, all day tomorrow, and all day Thursday.

—

An hour later.

"Gotta get going," My Friend says.

"What're you gonna do now?"

"Thought I'd Uber for a while." He's on his feet.

"Take a couple rides for me."

"No problem," he says, and he's out the door.

Gives me an opportunity to roll around with Jess. We both fall asleep. But I wake back up around midnight. Go back in the living room, get back to work for a couple hours.

Stretch out on the couch at 4 a.m.

Start watching The Godfather. Watch Bonasera the undertaker ask Don Vito Corleone for a favor. He tells Don Vito about the two bastards who took his daughter for a drive, made her drink whiskey, and tried to take advantage of her.

Last thing I remember is Bonasera saying, "They suspenda da sentence."

I wake back up at 6. The Godfather's still playing, near the end. When it ends, I click on Ray Donovan.

Back to work for two more hours.

Then back to the couch for some cat-napping.

—

Next time I open my eyes, Jess is walking in the door carrying a box from Dunkin Donuts. Plus two large coffees on one of those gray corrugated carriers.

"They didn't have blueberry," she says. "But I got a pretty good assortment. Should be something in there you like."

I hear her opening and closing cabinet doors. "Where do you keep your dishes?"

"Right on top of the microwave. Use as many as you want. They're unbreakable."

Less than a minute later we're sitting next to each other on the couch. Eating doughnuts off paper plates and drinking coffee out of Styrofoam cups. I'm working on an apple crumb when Jess notices my beat-up Eagles blanket on the floor.

"You slept on the couch?" she asks.

"For a while."

"Get much done?"

"Yep. But still more to do."

"Good," she says. "I'm going to work at the new place, so I might not be back all day. Call you when I know for sure."

"Good deal. I'll clean up."

She kisses my cheek on the way out.

"Thanks for the coffee and doughnuts."

"Any time." And she's gone.

—

Goes pretty much the same all the way to Thursday night.

The Blacklist is playing in the background. I'm not paying much attention because I'm putting the finishing touches on my story.

Chronology's fine. Characters well-rounded. Plenty of suspense and mystery. Satisfied with my plot points. Only thing left is dicking around with the theme.

Make myself a cup of coffee.

Jess walks in the door, kisses my cheek. "So where are you now?"

"Smoothing out the theme."

"What's theme?" she asks.

"Let's see. Are you a football fan?"

"I go to The Grog," she says, "to watch all the Eagles games. I go with Margo."

"With who?"

"You're not funny," she says.

"Anyway, the captains get together before the game starts. They flip a coin to see who's going to kick off."

"Who doesn't know that," she says.

"So let's say the Eagles are playing the Cowboys, and the game's here in Philly. The captains meet at the 50. Since the Cowboys are the visiting team, they get to call the flip."

"Who doesn't know that," she says again.

"Right. Like I was saying, the ref flips the coin and a Cowboy calls 'Heads.' But the coin lands on tails. So the Eagles get to decide if they wanta kickoff, receive, or defer."

"What do they decide to do?" she asks.

"Doesn't matter."

"Why not?" she asks.

"Got nothing to do with the theme."

"So what's the theme?" she says.

"If you'd just listen and quit interrupting, I'd tell you."

"So tell me," she says.

"Thank you. A sportswriter from Dallas says the Cowboys lost the toss. But a sportswriter from Philly says the Eagles won the toss. They're both describing the same event. The coin flip. That's the plot. But each sportswriter puts his own spin on it. That's theme. Get it?"

"Oh," she says. "Simple. Now I get it."

"Sounds simple, but it's complicated."

I turn back toward the computer.

Jess starts kissing my cheek again. But these are more than pecks.

"Can you take a break soon?" she says. "I was hoping we could, you know, do it."

CHAPTER 29

The next morning.

Bernie leads me into the courtroom. A wide aisle runs down the middle. Rows of chairs on both sides with scatterings of spectators. Jess and My Friend sitting on the left.

The bailiff steps in front of the bench, calls our case.

"Let's go." Bernie leads the way down the aisle. Sets his briefcase on the defense table, we sit.

The prosecutor's taking his position behind the prosecution table. Same prosecutor as before.

The judge asks them to identify themselves. Which they do. Then the prosecutor reads the charges against me.

"Mr. Wald," the judge says, "you have heard the charges against your client. Do you have any questions in regard to any of those charges?"

"No, your honor." Bernie stands. "We acknowledge the charges as read." He moves behind me, places both hands on my shoulders. "On behalf of Mr. Piasecki, who's sitting right in front of me, we ask the court to enter a plea of not guilty to all charges."

"So noted." She makes a note. "Are you ready to commence, Mr. Baldino?"

The prosecutor stands. "The Commonwealth calls Officer Edward Roth."

The officer takes the stand, testifies about responding to a 911-call at Media Station Apartments. In the bathroom of Apartment 201, in the bathtub, he observed the dead body of a white female. Notified C.I.D. headquarters about a possible drug overdose.

The prosecutor calls the medical examiner.

Dr. Nakamura describes the appearance of the body. Says he checked for vital signs. Found none, pronounced the victim dead at the scene.

"Did you specify a cause of death?"

"Accidental drug overdose."

"Please explain why," the prosecutor says.

"On the vanity next to the sink, in close proximity to the victim, I observed a small mirror. On that mirror, I observed a white powdery residue. I also observed one single-edge razor blade next to the mirror."

"Did you observe anything else in close proximity to the victim?"

"I also observed a small plastic baggie next to the mirror. A white powdery residue was visible on the inside of the baggie. It looked similar to the white powdery residue on the mirror."

"Did you subsequently identify the white powdery residue?"

"Our lab determined both residues to be fentanyl."

"For those of us unfamiliar with the term," the prosecutor says, "please educate us."

"Fentanyl is an extremely powerful opioid. Actually, a synthetic form of morphine, and significantly more potent than both morphine and heroin."

The prosecutor picks up some paperwork, approaches his witness. Hands him the paperwork.

"Dr. Nakamura, is this the lab report in question?"

He looks at the report. "Yes, it is."

"Commonwealth Exhibit One, your honor." The prosecutor hands the report to the judge.

She takes the report, looks at it. Passes it to the court clerk, who tags it, places it on a table in front of the bench.

"Now, Dr. Nakamura," the prosecutor says, "please describe that plastic baggie you found in close proximity to the victim."

"The letters U-B-E-R were stamped on the baggie in black."

This comes as quite a shock to me. But Bernie shows no change of emotion.

The prosecutor takes a plastic envelope off his table. Approaches the medical examiner, shows it to him.

"Dr. Nakamura, can you identify the document inside this plastic receptacle?"

"That is the baggie in question. The one trademarked with the Uber lettering."

"How can you be sure it's the same baggie?"

"I printed my initials in the lower right hand corner, very small, and there they are."

"Commonwealth Exhibit Two, your honor." The prosecutor hands the plastic envelope to the judge.

"So noted." The judge glances at it, makes a note. Passes it to her clerk for processing.

"Thank you, Dr. Nakamura. No more questions."

"Would you like to cross-examine?" the judge asks Bernie.

"Yes, your honor," Bernie responds. Glances at his notes. Stands, takes a step toward the witness.

"As I understand it, Dr. Nakamura, you testified that you sent the Uber baggie to the police lab for testing. Is that correct?"

"We sent the Uber baggie, the razor blade, and the–"

"Dr. Nakamura," Bernie interrupts, "please answer the specific question I just asked you. Did you send the Uber baggie to the police lab for testing? Yes or no?"

"Yes."

"Thank you," Bernie says. "To the best of your knowledge, did the police lab observe, and/or identify, *any* fingerprints, on the Uber baggie in question?"

"Not to the best of my knowledge."

"So there's no way to determine if the defendant, Mr. Piasecki, ever touched that baggie, is there?"

"No. But the baggie–"

"Dr. Nakamura," Bernie cuts him off again. "No unsolicited answers, please." Bernie grabs a document from our table. Glances at it, holds it up. "Dr. Nakamura, I see here that you later performed an autopsy on the victim. Is that correct?"

"Objection, your honor," the prosecutor interrupts. "I do not see any relevance to any questions in regard to an autopsy."

"Mr. Wald?" the judge says. "Please explain."

"Let me rephrase, your honor." Bernie looks at the document, reads for a moment. "It says here, that during the subsequent autopsy, you observed an injury to the victim's right wrist?"

"Objection, your honor," the prosecutor calls out. "I still see no relevance to any questions in regard to an autopsy, or the victim's right wrist."

"Mr. Wald," the judge says, "I'm perplexed as well."

"Your honor," Bernie says, "I will be calling Mr. Piasecki to the witness stand. His testimony will make this line of questioning abundantly clear."

"Very well," the judge says. "Objection overruled for the time being. Dr. Nakamura, please answer the question."

"If memory serves, I did observe an edema on the victim's wrist. The right wrist."

"And what is your expert opinion," Bernie asks, "about the cause of that trauma?"

"It was consistent with having been twisted."

"Thank you, Dr. Nakamura," Bernie says. "No more questions."

Dr. Nakamura steps down.

The prosecutor calls out, "The Commonwealth calls Salvatore Mazza."

A big, tough-looking guy comes forward. Swears to tell the truth, takes his place on the witness stand. Testifies that he worked with the victim on the night in question. Saw her leave work in an Uber vehicle.

Which, of course, is my vehicle.

"Thank you, Mr. Mazza. No more questions."

"Would you like to cross-examine?" the judge asks Bernie.

"Yes, your honor." Bernie stands. "As I understand it, Mr. Mazza, you're employed as a bouncer, is that correct?"

So that's who he is. The bouncer who twisted her wrist.

"Objection, your honor," the prosecutor says. "Mr. Mazza's occupation is not critical to the issue at hand."

"Objection sustained," the judge says.

"Okay," Bernie says. "But Mr. Mazza, it is true that you work at the Babes in Toyland strip club, is it not?"

"Objection, your honor," the prosecutor says. "Mr. Mazza's place of employment is not critical to the issue at hand either."

"*Au contraire*, Mr. Baldino," Bernie says. "I am trying to establish the starting point of the victim's ride home, from her place of employment. Which is indeed critical to this case."

"I will allow this latitude," the judge says. "Overruled."

"Thank you, your honor," Bernie says. "Now to be precise, Mr. Mazza, at your place of employment, Miss Forsythe danced around on a stage in scanty outfits ..."

"Objection, your honor," the prosecutor shouts.

"... twirled around on a pole, and stripped off her clothing in front of paying customers, did she not?"

"Objection, your honor," the prosecutor says again. "Mr. Wald is trying to demean the victim."

"If the shoe fits," Bernie says.

"Mr. Wald," the judge intervenes. "Enough. The victim is not on trial."

"Sorry, your honor," Bernie apologizes. "Mr. Mazza, at your place of employment, was the victim known as Rita Forsythe? Or did she go by a different name?"

"I'm not sure what ya mean."

"You know exactly what I mean, Mr. Mazza," Bernie says. "Miss Forsythe went by the stage name Jade, did she not?"

"Yeah."

"Just for the record, Mr. Mazza," Bernie says, "I notice two prominent red marks on your left cheek. I'm curious about how you acquired those marks?"

"Objection, your honor," the prosecutor says. "The marks on Mr. Mazza's face are not germane to this case."

"Maybe they're not," Bernie counters. "And, then again, maybe they are. In either case, your honor, I'd like to find out."

"You're pushing it, Mr. Wald," the judge says.

"This line of questioning will become abundantly clear when Mr. Piasecki testifies, your honor."

"In that case, I will overrule the objection, again for the time being, and allow Mr. Mazza to answer."

"Thank you, your honor," Bernie replies. "Once again, Mr. Mazza. How did you get those red marks on your left cheek?"

"I do judo."

"Interesting," Bernie says. "That could explain it. But prior to the time that Jade left the strip club, on the night in question, did you engage in any sort of altercation with her?"

"I'm not sure what ya mean."

"Once again, Mr. Mazza," Bernie says, "you know exactly what I mean. Did you engage in an altercation with Jade, a physical altercation in which you twisted her right wrist, judo style ..."

"Objection," the prosecutor calls out.

"... an altercation to which she retaliated by slapping you across the face, with a riding crop, not once, but twice?"

"Objection, your honor," the prosecutor says. "I don't see any relevance to this line of questioning."

"Mr. Wald?" the judge asks

"Your honor," Bernie says. "Once again the relevance will become readily obvious once Mr. Piasecki testifies."

"I hope so," the judge replies. "Because you are indeed pushing the envelope."

"Just one more question, your honor," Bernie says.

"Proceed," the judge says.

"Mr. Mazza," Bernie says, "was your altercation with Jade, the result of a disagreement, about the amount you charged her, for purchasing the bag of China White you sold her?"

"Objection," the prosecutor shouts.

"The bag of China White that killed her?"

"Objection sustained." The judge stares at Bernie. "Mr. Mazza is not on trial."

"But maybe he should be, your honor."

"Mr. Wald!"

"Question withdrawn," Bernie says. "I'm done with this guy, your honor."

The judge excuses the witness.

The bouncer steps down from the witness stand, glares at Bernie. Starts to leave. Veers toward Bernie, stops right next to him.

"What?" Bernie whispers. "You want to try some judo on me, tough guy?"

The bouncer grabs Bernie's wrist, twists his arm behind his back.

I jump right up. Try to break the bouncer's hold on Bernie. Some pushing and shoving ensue.

"Order in the court." The judge raps her gavel.

But the pushing and shoving continue until both bailiffs reach us, subdue the bouncer.

"I will not tolerate such outbursts in my courtroom," the judge says.

The bailiffs maintain a good grip on the bouncer.

I continue to stand in between him and Bernie.

"Mr. Mazza," the judge says, "I am holding you in contempt of court. Perhaps 24 hours behind bars will help you control your temper."

"That's bullshit," the bouncer fires back. "He started it with his big mouth."

"Make that 48 hours, Mr. Mazza."

That shuts the bouncer's mouth.

"Mr. Vanzant," the judge instructs one of the bailiffs, "please take Mr. Mazza into custody."

"Yes, your honor." The bailiff places handcuffs around the bouncer's wrists. Leads him out of the courtroom.

"Thanks," Bernie whispers to me.

"Are you gentlemen all right?" the judge asks Bernie.

"Yes, your honor," Bernie replies. "Thank you."

"Would you like a short recess?"

"No thank you, your honor. We're ready, willing, and able to continue."

"Mr. Baldino," the judge says, "please call your next witness."

"The Commonwealth calls Agent Frank Santangelo."

A cop-type, white, around 40, tall and stocky.

"In your own words, Agent Santangelo," the prosecutor says, "please explain the significance of the Uber lettering stamped on the drug baggie."

"Last year we identified a major drug dealer in New York City. A Mexican national calling himself the Cisco Kid. His full name is Francisco Zayas."

"What can you tell us about this individual?"

"He's part of the Sinaloa Cartel in Mexico, and he packages his product in Uber baggies just like the one in question."

"Please tell the court," the prosecutor says, "what you mean by product."

"Product is another term for illegal drugs."

"Why would a drug dealer," the prosecutor asks, "stamp his baggies in this fashion?"

"They like to trademark their baggies so the street-users know who the drugs are coming from. It's, like, their form of advertising."

"I see," the prosecutor says. "Is there any *other* reason why this Cisco Kid stamps the Uber lettering on his baggies?"

"He uses Uber drivers to distribute his product."

Wow, there's another shocker for me. Suddenly becoming clear why they think I supplied the drugs that killed her.

"Thank you, Agent Santangelo," the prosecutor says. "No more questions."

"Would you like to cross-examine?" the judge asks Bernie.

"Yes, your honor," Bernie responds. Glances at his notes as gets up. "Agent Santangelo, you mentioned a major drug dealer who operates out of New York City. And you said he delivers his product in baggies stamped with the Uber lettering. Is that correct?"

"Yes, sir."

"And you also said," Bernie says, "that this major drug dealer uses Uber drivers to distribute his product. Is that also correct?"

"Yes, sir."

"I see," Bernie says. "So, to the best of your knowledge, is there any drug cartel currently operating in the Philadelphia area, that uses Uber drivers to distribute its product?"

"We believe that may be the case."

"Agent Santangelo," Bernie says, "I did not ask you, what you, or what the DEA, *may believe*. Can you document, that even one Uber driver in the Philadelphia area, is distributing any sort of drugs, in baggies stamped with Uber lettering?"

"No, sir."

"Not even one driver?" Bernie verifies.

"No."

"And definitely not the defendant, Mr. Piasecki. Is that also correct?"

"That's correct."

"Thank you, Agent Santangelo. No more questions."

The judge excuses the witness, calls for a short recess.

—

We have 15 minutes to get together in a conference room. Bernie asks Jess and My Friend to join us for moral support.

But neither ever went to a criminal court before. No idea how my ordeal's proceeding. Nor do I.

"Bernie," I say, "I had no idea about the Uber baggie, or about Uber drivers delivering drugs. How bad does that make me look?"

"Looks bad from where I'm sitting," My Friend says.

"Sure does," Jess says.

"If a jury were involved," Bernie says, "it would paint you with an implication of guilt, like you're friends just commented. But we're not dealing with a jury at this point. The only one we have to convince is the judge."

"Can you do that?" I ask.

"That's why I trashed the bouncer like that. To plant seeds of doubt. To make it look like he's the supplier, not you. To create reasonable doubt."

"Do you think it worked?"

"Time will tell."

—

Court resumes.

The prosecutor calls Det. Pamela Bishop.

She's one of the detectives who arrested me. She comes forward. Swears the oath, settles into the witness box.

"Det. Bishop," the prosecutor begins, "in your own words, please tell us how you became involved with the case."

"My partner and I responded to a 911-call at Media Station Apartments. Dr. Nakamura was already on the scene, attending to a dead white female in the bathtub. He already pronounced the victim dead of an accidental drug overdose."

"Please describe the scene for the court."

"Dr. Nakamura pointed out drug paraphernalia in close proximity to the victim. One item was a plastic baggie with a white powdery residue visible inside the baggie. In addition, the Uber lettering was visible on the outside of the baggie."

"Det. Bishop," the prosecutor says, "the Uber baggie in question has already been introduced as evidence in this case. Please tell the court how the defendant," points directly at my face, "who is sitting right there, fits into this case."

"He's the Uber driver," she says, "that picked up the victim at her place of employment, and transported her to her residence."

"Was the defendant present at the time of the discovery of the body?"

"No, sir," she says. "He was not."

"Then how is it you came to identify him?"

"I spoke with two of the victim's coworkers," she says. "They came to check on her well-being. From them, I learned they all worked together at the Babes in Toyland gentlemen's club in South Philadelphia."

"And from there?" the prosecutor says.

"Objection, your honor," Bernie calls out. "He's leading the witness."

"Sustained," the judge says. "Please rephrase, Mr. Baldino."

"Det. Bishop," the prosecutor rephrases, "was that information helpful in any way?"

"Yes, sir."

"How was it helpful?"

"It gave us a starting point. And, subsequently, my partner and I visited the gentlemen's club and interviewed the manager. He referred us to a member of his security personnel, who told us he saw the victim leave the club in an Uber."

"Was that individual able to identify the driver?"

"No, sir."

"How did you identify the driver?"

"We contacted the Uber hub in Southwest Philadelphia and learned that the driver's name was Steve Piasecki. They keep current photos of their drivers, and we obtained a recent photo of him."

"So," the prosecutor asks, "did you then just assume that this defendant was, in fact, the Uber driver who transported Miss Forsythe home? Based solely on Uber's say-so?"

"No, sir. We did not."

"How then did you verify that the defendant," pointing at me again, "is, in fact, the Uber driver who transported Miss Forsythe home on the night in question?"

"We made arrangements with the manager of the Media Station Apartments to view the security video from the night in question."

"And did you?" the prosecutor asks.

"We did. We went to the manager's office and watched the video."

"What, if anything," the prosecutor asks, "did you observe on said video?"

"We observed a white female approaching the entrance to the building. She was followed closely by a white male who appeared to be carrying a small case and two shopping bags."

"Were you able to identify either individual in that video?"

"We were able to positively identify the female as the victim, Miss Rita Forsythe. And based on the photo we received from Uber, we believed the white male to be Steve Piasecki."

"You used the term believed," the prosecutor says. "Were you subsequently able to confirm your belief?"

"We were."

"How?"

"We previously obtained his address from Uber, so my partner and I visited his place of residence."

"Did you then see the defendant," pointing at me again, "at his place of residence, face to face, with your own eyes?"

"My partner and I both did."

"Was this defendant," again pointing at me, "the white male you observed on the video from the Media Station Apartments?"

"He was."

"How can you be so sure?"

"When we saw him at his apartment, it was apparent to both my partner and myself that he was, in fact, the white male we saw in that security video."

"Was there any other way?"

"He confirmed his name, and he also confirmed the fact that he transported Miss Forsythe from her place of work to her residence."

"Thank you, Det. Bishop. I have no more questions."

The prosecutor sits down.

"Mr. Wald," the judge says, "would you like to cross examine the witness?"

"No questions at this time, your honor," Bernie says.

"Thank you, Det. Bishop," the judge says. "You are excused."

Det. Bishop steps down from the witness stand. Exits through the gate, walks toward the back of the courtroom.

"Mr. Baldino," the judge says, "are you ready to call your next witness?"

"That was my last witness, your honor."

"Mr. Wald," the judge says, "I believe you plan to call on the defendant to testify. Is that correct?"

"Yes, your honor."

"And I anticipate that he will be on the witness stand for a considerable amount of time. Is that also correct?"

"Yes, your honor."

"In that case," she says, "rather than risk interrupting his testimony, we will take a short recess. Court will resume in 15 minutes."

She raps her gavel.

CHAPTER 30

Court resumes.

"Mr. Wald," the judge addresses Bernie, "are you ready to call your first witness?"

"The defense calls Mr. Steven Piasecki."

I stand, make the short walk from the defense table to the witness stand.

The bailiff's waiting with a Bible.

I place my left hand on the Bible, raise my right hand. Swear to tell the truth, the whole truth, and nothing but the truth, so help me God.

I take my place in the witness box.

"Mr. Piasecki," Bernie begins, "are you employed?"

"Not at the present."

"Interesting." Bernie feigns surprise. "But you were employed on the night in question, is that correct?"

"That's correct."

"How were you employed on the night in question?"

"I worked as an Uber driver."

"I see," Bernie says. "Between then and now, did something happen that curtailed your ability to work as an Uber driver?"

"Yes."

"Did you quit?" Bernie asks.

"No, sir."

"What happened?" Bernie asks.

"Uber suspended my driving privileges."

"For what reason?" Bernie asks.

"They sent an email, informing me that I was suspended because of, well ..." I open my arms, extend them outward to indicate what's taking place in the courtroom. "... because of this."

"To clarify, Mr. Piasecki," Bernie says, "you say that Uber informed you, via email, that you were suspended, because you have been falsely accused–"

"Objection, your honor," the prosecutor protests. "This process will determine whether or not Mr. Piasecki has been falsely accused of anything. However, the Commonwealth asserts that he is guilty of all charges for which he's been accused. Moreover, this case will not be decided by my adversary's blatant grandstanding."

"Objection sustained," the judge rules.

"Blatant grandstanding notwithstanding," Bernie retorts, "Mr. Piasecki, you are no longer gainfully employed, is that correct?"

"That's correct. I am not."

"Let's go back," Bernie says, "to when you were still working as an Uber driver. In fact, let's go back to the night in question. Did you, or did you not, transport Miss Rita Forsythe, from her place of employment, to her residence?"

"I did. But I didn't know her by that name. She identified herself as Jade."

"I see," Bernie says. "Had you at any time in your life, previously met, or previously known, the individual you transported from her place of employment, to her residence, on the night in question?"

"No, sir."

"So she was a complete stranger to you?"

"Yes, sir. She was."

"What, if anything," Bernie asks, "happened during the ride in question?"

"A few things happened."

"Oh?" Bernie acts surprised. "Like what?"

"To begin with, I try to avoid having conversations with strippers. Strippers and hookers."

"Objection, your honor," the prosecutor calls out. "I object to the witness categorizing Miss Forsythe in such a manner."

"Well, Mr. Baldino," Bernie challenges, "what is the proper terminology, for individuals who dance in front of random strangers, and take their clothes off?"

"Enough bickering, gentlemen," the judge intervenes. "Mr. Wald, please instruct your witness to use different terminology in regard to the employment of the victim."

"Certainly, your honor," Bernie responds. "Would exotic dancer be permissible?"

"That's fine," the judge says.

"So Mr. Piasecki," Bernie says, "what were you saying before being interrupted by the prosecutor."

"I try to avoid conversations with exotic dancers."

"And why is that?" Bernie asks.

"I don't want to engage in any conversations that might be misconstrued in any way, shape, or form, as off-color, or sexual in nature or content."

"Why?" Bernie asks.

"I don't want any complaints that might jeopardize my job."

"With that in mind," Bernie says, "did you, or did you not, have a conversation, with this exotic dancer, on the night in question?"

"I did."

"Why?" Bernie asks.

"She initiated a conversation."

"What was the nature of the conversation?"

"She told me about having a confrontation with an old boyfriend just prior to leaving the club."

"Did your rider happen to identify her old boyfriend?"

"She did."

"Is it anyone we might know?" Bernie asks.

"It is."

"Who is it?" Bernie asks.

"One of the witnesses who testified earlier."

"Really?" Bernie says. "Which witness?"

"I believe his last name is Mazza."

"Well-well-well," Bernie says. "What do you know about that?" Pauses. "How did Mr. Mazza's name come up in conversation that night?"

"She referred to him as Sal. So I never heard his last name until he was called as a witness here today."

"I understand," Bernie says. "Once again, how did this Sal's name come up in the victim's conversation with you?"

"She said he offered to drive her home, but she refused. Then he tried to bully her. So she picked up her riding crop and whipped him across the face. Not once, but twice."

"Interesting," Bernie says. "That seems to explain those two red marks on Mr. Mazza's face. Did Jade say whether or not that whipping ended their altercation?"

"She said he grabbed her wrist and twisted it behind her back with a judo hold. She said he kept twisting her wrist until he forced her to drop the whip."

"Did she mention any injury she sustained as a result of the altercation?"

"She said he sprained her wrist. Her right wrist."

"Mr. Piasecki," Bernie says, "did you hear Dr. Nakamura testify earlier that he observed the victim's right wrist to be traumatized as a result of being twisted?"

"Yes, sir. I did."

"Mr. Piasecki," Bernie asks, "what, if anything, happened when you arrived at your rider's residence?"

"Her wrist was sore and swollen by then. And she asked me to help carry her things?"

"And did you help?" Bernie asks.

"I did. I carried her belongings."

"Exactly how far did you carry her belongings?" Bernie asks.

"First, I carried them to her apartment building."

"Did you enter her building at that time?"

"I entered the foyer and carried them up one flight of stairs. Then I set her belongings on the floor outside her door."

"Did you then enter her apartment?"

"No, I did not. I went back down the stairs, and went back to work."

"I see," Bernie says. "Did you, on that night, or any occasion, enter her apartment?"

"No, sir. I never set one foot inside her apartment."

"Mr. Piasecki," Bernie asks, "in any of your conversations with the victim, did she mention anything about purchasing drugs from Sal Mazza?"

"Objection," the prosecutor shouts. "Mr. Mazza is not on trial."

"Perhaps he should be," Bernie says.

"Objection sustained," the judge says. "We already visited this, Mr. Wald. I already slapped contempt charges on Mr. Mazza. Would you like to spend 48 hours in the cooler with him?"

"No, your honor," Bernie says. "Sorry, your honor."

"Please proceed," she instructs Bernie.

"Mr. Piasecki," Bernie continues, "let's cut to the chase. Did you ever possess the drugs in question?"

"No, sir."

"Did you ever sell any drugs to Miss Forsythe?"

"No, sir."

"Thank you, Mr. Piasecki." Bernie turns to face the prosecutor. "Mr. Baldino, the witness is all yours."

"No questions," the prosecutor says.

"You may step down," the judge instructs me.

I return to my seat behind the defense table.

"Mr. Wald," the judge says, "are you ready to call your next witness?"

"No more witnesses, your honor."

"At this time," the judge asks, "is there a request from either party for pretrial conference?"

"Your honor," the prosecutor says, "the Commonwealth would be amenable to pretrial conference."

"One moment please, your honor," Bernie says, "to confer with my client."

"Granted," the judge says.

Bernie leans close to me, whispers, "They're hoping to make a deal with you."

"What kind of deal?"

"This is both assumption on my part," he says, "and speculation. But I believe they'd be willing to grant you immunity from prosecution in exchange for identifying the individuals operating the drug ring."

"Bernie, I already told you. I don't know anything about any drug ring."

Bernie gets back on his feet. "Your honor," he says, "we respectfully decline the offer for pretrial conference."

"For the record," the judge says, "the defendant waives his opportunity to schedule pretrial conference." She makes a note, looks at the prosecutor. "Mr. Baldino, are you ready for a summation?"

"Yes, your honor," the prosecutor stands.

"Your honor," Bernie interrupts, "I would like to submit a motion at this time?"

"What kind of motion, Mr. Wald?"

"I move for a judgment of acquittal."

"Objection," the prosecutor says.

"On what grounds, Mr. Wald?" the judge asks.

"Under Rule 606 of the Pennsylvania Rules of Criminal Procedure, the Commonwealth must establish a *prima facie* case. But the prosecution has yet to produce even one piece of *prima facie* evidence to prove that Mr. Piasecki committed any sort of crime whatsoever, or that he did anything illegal whatsoever."

"The Commonwealth," the prosecutor says, "submitted an abundance of *prima facie* evidence."

"*Au contraire*, Mr. Baldino," Bernie says. "All your witnesses have been consistent in testifying to certain facts, and to those certain facts only. One, the victim was found in her apartment, in her bathroom, in her bathtub, dead from a drug overdose. Two, a drug baggie trademarked with Uber lettering was found in close proximity to the victim's body. Three, on the night of the victim's demise, she was transported from her place of employment to her residence in an Uber. And four, by sheer coincidence, Mr. Piasecki was the Uber driver who transported the victim home."

"That sounds like enough evidence to me, your honor," the prosecutor says.

"But not to me," Bernie says. "The Fourth Amendment of the United States Constitution protects its citizens against unlawful arrest. And when it comes to criminal defense, these Fourth Amendment protections are both fundamental and foundational. The prosecution needs more than hunches and/or suspicions. But that's all you have, Mr. Baldino, hunches and/or suspicions, and you know it. In addition, your honor, the prosecution must have probable cause *before* making an arrest."

"We had probable cause," the prosecutor says.

"Did you?" Bernie differs. "Let's take the charges against Mr. Piasecki one at a time and put them all to the test. Charge number one is possession of a controlled substance. Mr. Baldino, you failed to provide even one witness who, in any way shows, let alone proves, that Mr. Piasecki ever possessed any drug whatsoever."

Bernie moves to the defense table, picks up a report. Spins back around to face the judge.

"In regard to the charge of possession of a controlled substance with intent to distribute. The search of Mr. Piasecki's apartment failed to discover even one baggie of the type usually associated with the distribution of drugs. Therefore, there was not one baggie found that was stamped with the Uber lettering. The search also failed to find even one scale of the type usually associated with the distribution of drugs. In fact, the search party failed to find as much as a bathroom scale in Mr. Piasecki's apartment."

A few snickers circle around the courtroom, making the judge rap her gavel to restore order.

"I submit this document as Defense Exhibit One, your honor," Bernie says. "It's a notarized copy of the search warrant executed at Mr. Piasecki's apartment."

The bailiff steps up to Bernie, takes the report. Carries it over to the bench, hands it to the judge.

"Please note, your honor," Bernie follows up. "The search found nothing even remotely associated with illegal drugs, or illegal drug activities."

The judge inspects the report for a good while.

"So noted." The judge passes the report to her clerk for processing.

"And when it comes to finding large amounts of cash," Bernie continues. "In Mr. Piasecki's kitchen, inside a Styrofoam cup, the search party found exactly, 7 dollars and 97 cents, in pennies, nickels, dimes, and quarters."

More snickers circle the courtroom, making the judge rap her gavel once again.

"Now let's take a look at the final charge against Mr. Piasecki," Bernie says. "Sale of a controlled substance. Your honor, it's impossible to sell something you never possessed. In regard to this charge, the prosecution has failed, in every way imaginable, to produce anyone, who witnessed Mr. Piasecki sell any controlled substances, to anyone, at any time. So accordingly, your honor, I move for an acquittal of all charges against Mr. Piasecki."

"On what basis?" the prosecutor demands.

"Commonwealth's Penal Code 225," Bernie says. "Rule 404. The circumstantial evidence before this court is insufficient to sustain a conviction, even when factoring in the watered-down burden of proof in preliminary hearings such as this. The Commonwealth has failed to present sufficient evidence, to make it look more likely that Mr. Piasecki committed the crimes for which he's been accused, rather than less likely."

The judge lapses into deep thought.

"Mr. Baldino," she eventually asks, "do you have any additional evidence to present to the court at this time?"

The prosecutor puts his head down. Starts looking at his notes, leafing through several documents on the table.

Nearly a minute passes in silence.

"Your honor?" Bernie breaks the silence.

"Mr. Baldino?" the judge says.

The prosecutor looks at the judge. "I have no additional evidence at this time, your honor."

Nearly another minute transpires while the judge deliberates.

"Judgment for acquittal is granted," she says. "All charges are dismissed. Mr. Piasecki, you are free to go." She raps her gavel to end the hearing.

"The Commonwealth objects to your decision, your honor," the prosecutor says. "We thus inform the court that we plan to file an appeal of your ruling."

"Check your law books, Mr. Baldino," the judge says. "You're embarrassing yourself. There are no appeals in a dismissal of charges at a preliminary hearing. If you wish to go forward with the charges against Mr. Piasecki, you must refile and seek out another judge to hear your case."

I can't stop shaking Bernie's hand and smiling.

CHAPTER 31

Less than an hour later.

The prosecutor's rushing down the corridor leading to the district attorney's office. He looks driven.

The private secretary's nowhere to be seen.

He opens the door and bursts inside.

The DA's taking a bite from a half-eaten sandwich. He sees the prosecutor. Sets the sandwich on top of a deli wrapper, next to five or six potato chips.

"I want to refile," the prosecutor asserts.

The DA looks at him, picks up his coffee. "You want to refile?" Takes a sip of his coffee, keeps holding the cup.

"Bob," the prosecutor says, "I take full responsibility for what happened today."

"You take full responsibility?" The DA cocks his head. "You take full responsibility for not knowing you can't appeal the dismissal of charges at a preliminary hearing?"

The prosecutor doesn't respond.

"That's inexcusable," the DA says.

"A stupid oversight on my part. I fucked up."

"You sure as fuck did," the DA says. "Hank, you're supposed to be my ace, but Bernie Fuckin' Wald turned you into a joker today. And now you're acting like a fucking wild man."

"I'm no fucking wild man," the prosecutor shouts like a wild man. "But this guy's guilty. And he's not just guilty of dealing drugs. He killed that girl. I know he did. We have to refile to get him off the street while we put the homicide together."

"Please tell me nothing slipped out in court today about the homicide."

"At one point," the prosecutor says, "I was afraid it might. That fucker brought up the autopsy. Twice. But I squelched it both times. But, Bob, we have to refile."

"No way I'm going to refile," the DA says, "just to make you feel better about yourself."

"But I'll win this time."

"How?" the DA says. "You have no tangible evidence. Not one witness."

"I'll work with C.I.D., Bob. We'll get more than enough."

"I'm not going to refile," the DA says, "and that's final."

"He killed that woman. Are you going to turn your back and let this guy get away with murder?"

CHAPTER 32

I park ten blocks from my apartment.

Jess, My Friend, and I get out of my Envoy, cross the street. We're going to the Broadway Bar.

I let them go first, then enter.

"Hey, Steve."

"Tony, how ya doin'?" He's the owner, in his 40s, and he gives me a strong handshake. "We've been expecting you."

I introduce him to Jess. He and My Friend already exchanged greetings.

"Bernie and Roy are here already." Tony points toward a small alcove off to the left. The room's dark and paneled. Framed photographs to commemorate the town's history cover the walls.

I'm wondering who Roy is.

Two rectangular tables are pushed together in the middle of the room. Bernie's seated on the near side with his back facing us. Another man, around the same age as Bernie, is seated on the other side of the table. Obviously Roy.

"Mike," Bernie says, "you already know Roy."

My Friend nods at Roy.

Bernie introduces Roy to Jess and me. He's Bernie's private investigator.

—

Ten minutes later.

We're eating and drinking. Food's good, the conversation's lively.

"Bernie," I say, "you were magnificent."

"Just doing my job," Bernie replies.

"You sounded just like my high school principal," Jess says, "when you told that Dr. What's-his-name—"

"Dr. Nakamura," Bernie interjects.

"Right." Jess changes her voice to imitate her principal, "Please answer the specific question I just asked you."

"And then you got him again," My Friend says. "No more unsolicited answers please."

We're all laughing.

"I was surprised," I say, "when you brought up the autopsy."

"That's all Roy's doing," Bernie says. "I wanted to lay some foundation about the sprained wrist." He looks at Roy. "Tell them."

Roy sets his drink down.

"I went down to the strip club," Roy says, "and spoke with the manager. They're always a little on the defensive in those kinds of places. You know, when a private dick drops in and starts asking questions. They always have some sort of shady shit going."

"The manager," Bernie says, "didn't quite give us what we needed. So Roy kept pushing. Tell them."

"The manager turned me onto the bouncer," Roy says. "Now that's one fucking knucklehead. He must have a lot of shit he's trying to hide because he told me everything. Even acted it out right in front of my eyes. Demonstrated the wrist lock on me, but gently."

We all laugh.

"Just like he tried on Bernie," My Friend says.

We laugh harder.

"Are you okay?" Jess asks Bernie.

"Thanks to your boyfriend," Bernie says.

"It was nothing," I say. "But getting back to the autopsy report—"

Bernie and Roy start laughing again.

"What's so funny?" I ask.

"Tell them," Bernie tells Roy.

"Over the years," Roy begins, "I cultivated contacts here and there. As fate would have it, one of those contacts works at the morgue. So I was able to find out about the autopsy, about the sprained wrist, and a whole lot more."

Bernie and Roy start laughing a little harder.

"Come on," I say. "Tell us what's so funny?"

"Tell them," Bernie tells Roy.

"Okay," Roy says. "Well, my contact at the morgue *told* me what happened, but he never *gave* me the autopsy report."

"But I saw it," Steve says.

"We all saw it," Jess says.

My Friend nods.

"You all saw *something*," Bernie says. "But you never saw me introduce the autopsy report as evidence, did you?"

"No," I say. "Why not?"

"I'm taking a vacation in two weeks," Bernie says. "Going to Argentina. My first trip to South America. I'm going to Buenos Aires."

"So?" I say.

"So I wasn't holding up the autopsy report," Bernie says. "I was holding up the itinerary for my trip to Buenos Aires."

"No shit," I say. "That's fuckin' hilarious."

We're all laughing when Tony and the bartender walk over. Tony's carrying a bottle of champagne. The bartender's carrying a tray with five champagne glasses.

"We have three more bottles on ice," Tony says.

We all thank him.

Tony pops the cork. The bartender sets the glasses on the table. Tony starts filling them.

"You're not joining us, Tony?" Bernie asks.

"Love to," the owner says. "But it's a long way to closing time. Plus this is your celebration."

Tony and the bartender leave.

The champagne keeps flowing for almost an hour. And the discussion keeps going.

We talk about the way Bernie handled the medical examiner. How he scorched Sal the bouncer. Provoked him into initiating the wrestling match. How he soft-balled the DEA agent into admitting no evidence existed against me. And the way Bernie turned my testimony into a masterpiece.

"I'd like to propose a toast." I lift my glass. "Here's to Buenos Aires."

"To Buenos Aires," the others echo. We all click glasses and sip our champagne.

But then I go silent. Start staring at the far wall.

Bernie notices. "What's wrong?"

"Something just hit me."

"What?"

"Roy's leaving something out."

"Like what?" Bernie says.

"Like, he said he learned a whole lot more at the morgue. But he never said what more he learned."

Bernie and Roy stare at each other.

"Well?" I break the silence.

Roy nods at Bernie.

"Okay," Bernie says. "This whole drug rigamarole was an exercise to keep us busy chasing our tails."

"Why?"

"The stripper didn't die from a drug overdose," Bernie says. "The autopsy proves somebody strangled her."

"And they think it was me?"

"Correct," Bernie says. "They think you used the drugs to disguise the fact you strangled her."

"Still?"

Bernie nods. "Most likely."

"So why are we celebrating like this?"

"You didn't kill her," Bernie says, "did you?"

"Fuck no."

"Then you have nothing to worry about," he says. "If they couldn't put the drug case together, no way they can put the homicide together.

They'll figure that out real quick. Plus I'll have a heart-to-heart with the DA and set him straight. You have nothing to worry about."

I keep staring at the wall for several seconds.

"Somebody killed that woman," I finally say, "and that somebody's getting away with murder?"

CHAPTER 33

Jess and I take an Uber home. In addition to drinking our fair share of champagne, I drank two bottles of Bud. Jess had a couple Margaritas, plus at least two shots of Cuervo. No way we're risking a DUI.

Four minutes after the ride starts at the Broadway, it ends at my apartment.

"I'll tip you on the app," I tell a man named Guwame who speaks with an African accent.

Jess and I are out the door of his Honda Accord.

We're holding hands as we enter my building. We walk up two flights. Pass through the fire door. Take a few more steps to reach my apartment, stop outside the door.

I start digging for my keys. "Here they are." I unlock the door, open it for Jess.

The screensaver's playing. I step over to the coffee table.

"Where do you think you're going, big boy," Jess says.

I pick up the remote. Make a few clicks, switch to an episode of Ray Donovan.

"Are we going to do it?" She's standing in a straddling posture. Sticking her chest out provocatively at the same time. "Or what?"

She looks imposing and sexy at the same time.

"You better believe it." I set the remote back on top of the coffee table. "Just wanta check my email first."

"What?" She's staring at me.

"I'll be really fast. Just wanta see if I got anything from Rose."

"Who's Rose?" she asks.

"Editor-in-chief of the magazine."

"Oh." She takes off her top. "Does Rose look like this?"

"You win. Let's go."

We never make it past the couch.

CHAPTER 34

I wake up on the couch, but Jess is gone. It's morning. She musta gone to work at that new place again.

As happy as I am to see the drug charges dropped, it bothers me that C.I.D. still thinks I murdered the dead stripper.

I wanta prove my innocence, but have no idea how. Then something hits me like a ton of bricks.

All of a sudden I'm feeling like Jessica Fletcher from Murder, She Wrote. Like her, I'm a mystery writer, except for the fact I'm still an *unpublished* mystery writer. Still, just like her, I decide to help the police solve a murder case.

—

I take an Uber back to the Broadway to pick up my Envoy.

Next, I'm driving down a hill. Turning into the Media Station Apartments. Driving up a hill. A right turn takes me to the far end of the A Building. I park, then approach the entrance.

I thought about what button to push all the way here. The dead stripper lived in Apartment 201. There are four apartments on each floor. Two on one side of the landing, two on the other. Her landing has doors to Apartments 200, 201, 202, and 203.

If numbered consecutively, her next-door neighbor lives in 202. But if they're odd on one side, even on the other, then she lives in 203.

So is it 202? Or 203?

I climb the steps. Stop. Look down at the panel of buttons. Play a hunch and press 203.

Five seconds later a woman's voice says, "Yes?"

"Ma'am, we don't know each other, but it's very important that I see you."

"About what?"

"About your next-door neighbor."

No response. And no more hollow sound coming out of the speaker.

I press 203 again.

"Go away, sir," comes out of the speaker, "or I'll call the police."

"Ma'am, please. You can do that but, like I said, it's very important that I talk to you."

"Who are you?"

"Ma'am, I know your neighbor's dead. I just want to talk to you about her death."

"You're one of those snoopy reporters," she says, "aren't you."

"No, I'm–" That's as far as I get. She's gone again.

I press 203 and hold it down.

"That's it, sir," she says. "I warned you. Now I'm calling–"

"Since you're so into my shit, why don't you come over and trim my pussy hair next time it needs trimming."

—

The door to Apartment 203 opens. I see a middle-aged white female. I was expecting the spinster-look, but she's dressed well enough to enter any restaurant in town.

"State your case fast, mister," she says, "or you get the door in your face."

"My name's Steve. I'm the Uber driver who drove your neighbor home that night. You know, the night before she was found dead in the bathtub."

"Go on."

"The police accused me of being the drug dealer who supplied the drugs that killed her."

"Did they arrest you?"

"Yes, they did."

"Then why aren't you in jail?"

"Because I'm innocent."

"That's what they all say."

"Ma'am, I went to court, and I was exonerated."

"So why are you here now?"

"Your neighbor didn't die of a drug overdose."

"What are you talking about?"

"Someone murdered her, Ma'am. I'd like to find out who, and I think you can help me."

"How?"

"I know about your camera."

"Ruth," she says. "Please call me Ruth. Ma'am makes me feel old."

—

Two minutes later.

We're sitting in her living room. Nicely furnished. She's on the sofa. I'm in an end chair. She offers coffee, but I politely decline.

"So, Steve," she says, "how exactly can I help you solve this, this, this murder case, you say?"

"This is a shot in the dark, Ruth. But I'm hoping you still have your recordings from that night."

She smiles, stands. "Come with me."

She leads me into the dining area, to a desk against one wall. She's got an old Packard Bell computer. A relic. With a large monitor sitting on top of the processor box, an external keyboard, and the computer tower on the floor underneath the desk.

"Pull up a chair." She sits at the desk. "I keep everything on floppies. Everything since I moved in here three years ago."

She turns on the computer.

I take a chair from under the dining room table, swing it around. Pull it up next to her, take a seat.

She opens a container of floppies, starts thumbing through. "Easy enough." She pulls out a floppy. Reaches down, inserts it inside a slot in the tower.

The monitor warms up and we're ready to go.

"I dropped her off a little before midnight," I say.

The video start playing. She starts scanning forward. "Should be right around here." She hits **STOP**, then **PLAY**, and we start watching.

We're looking at an empty landing for almost a minute. She fast forwards a little more, and bingo. The door opens, the dead stripper enters the landing. Here I come, right behind, carrying the makeup case and two shopping bags.

"There you are, Steve," Ruth says. "Why are you carrying those things?"

"She had an argument before she left the club. An old boyfriend. He twisted her wrist and it hurt her too much to carry anything."

"Well," she says, "aren't you Sir Galahad."

One at a time, I hand the dead stripper her belongings. She sets them inside her apartment. Looks like she thanks me, then closes the door. I turn to leave.

"You didn't even go inside," she says.

"Nope."

"So you think if we keep watching this," she says, "we're going to see the killer."

"Very perceptive. He had to get here sometime after I left."

"This is so exciting," she says. "I can't wait."

"Shouldn't take long. Another car was coming in as I was leaving. I believe our man was driving that car."

She fast forwards. Not for long. We see some activity. She reverses the video to where the activity starts, hits **PLAY**.

An older man's coming through the door. Around 50. Not wearing a suit, but dressed well. We get a good look at his face as he walks up to the dead stripper's apartment.

He taps on the door once. The door opens a moment later. The dead stripper's wearing a bathrobe. He steps inside, the door closes.

"I never saw him before," she says. "Is that our killer?"

—

Up the courthouse steps. Through a revolving door, down a flight of steps. I know my way around C.I.D. headquarters. Already been here twice this week.

Enter the waiting room carrying my laptop. No one else is waiting. I step right up to the reception window, see a female in uniform on the other side of the glass.

"How can I help you, sir?" she asks.

"I'd like to see Det. Bishop."

"Is she expecting you?"

"No."

"Who should I say is calling?"

"Mr. Piasecki."

"Please take a seat, sir, while I try to contact her."

I step back. Move over to the right, take a seat.

Less than two minutes pass.

A door opens, Det. Bishop steps into the waiting room. She has to be surprised to see me, but it doesn't show.

She approaches me.

I stand up.

"Mr. Piasecki, how exactly can I help you?"

I wait until we come face to face.

"The way I hear it, you folks think I murdered the dead stripper."

—

I'm sitting in the same Interrogation Room where she and her partner interrogated me earlier in the week. I'm on one side of a small table. She's on the other side.

We didn't talk on the short walk from the waiting room.

"What would make you say something like that?" she begins.

"Let's quit fucking around." My frankness surprises her. "I know about the autopsy." More surprise on her face. "I know someone strangled her."

"You have my attention, Mr. Piasecki."

"About fuckin' time." I'm enjoying this acting out, by the way. My form of payback. But enough's enough. Time to get down to business.

"On the night I transported her home," I continue, "a car passed me as I was pulling away from the entrance to her building. BMW, dark-colored. I believe the killer was driving that car. Should I go on?"

"Please continue," she says.

"When I drove her home, she talked a lot. Told me about a nosey neighbor. A nosey neighbor with a security camera. Just three hours ago I paid a visit to that nosey neighbor. Believe it or not, she kept the video from that night. She and I just watched it. We watched the killer enter her apartment and leave an hour later."

—

Four hours later.

Instead of being followed by an unmarked car, I'm now following an unmarked car. My new partner-in-crime, Ruth, is riding shotgun.

We follow the unmarked car to a ritzy section of Chestnut Hill. We're driving along a narrow road, passing trees and fields off to the right, well-tended mansions off to the left.

We reach a mansion sitting all by itself on top of a decent-sized hill. The unmarked car turns into the driveway. We turn, keep following.

The winding drive leads uphill for a good quarter-mile. The unmarked car stops, we stop.

We watch Det. Bishop and Det. Chase exit the unmarked car, approach the entrance to the mansion.

CHAPTER 35

The front door of the mansion opens to reveal a uniformed butler.

"How can I help you?" the butler asks.

"We're here to see Judge Wesley," Det. Bishop says.

"And who shall I say is calling?"

"I'm Det. Bishop with the Delaware County C.I.D." She presents her credentials. "And this is my partner Det. Chase."

Det. Chase flashes his badge.

"Please step inside." The butler indicates a large vestibule immediately inside the entrance. He waits for the detectives to step inside, then closes the door. "I will inform the judge of your presence." He walks away.

"Did you ever see Gone with the Wind?" Det. Chase says as his eyes wander around.

"Tell me about it." She's all eyes as well.

Judge Winston Wesley joins them less than two minutes later. Medium-sized man, 52 years old, with a tanned face from regular rounds of golf at the nearby Philadelphia Cricket Club.

"I don't believe we've ever met before," the judge says.

"I'm Det. Bishop with the Delaware County C.I.D., and this is my partner Det. Chase."

"I see," the judge says. "How exactly can I help you folks?"

"We'd like you to accompany us to C.I.D. headquarters," Det. Bishop says.

The judge furrows his brow. "And what is the reason for such a request?"

"We'd like to discuss your whereabouts," Det. Bishop says, "on the night of March 7th, a Wednesday, and/or the early morning hours of March 8th."

"I rarely go out at night," the judge says. "Especially on weeknights. So I'm sure I was right here."

"We have reason to believe otherwise," Det. Bishop says.

"I'm sure I have no idea what you're talking about," the judge says. "And I would like to have the name of your superior, please."

"Look, Judge Wesley," Det. Chase says. "We can do this the easy way, or we can do it the hard way. The choice is yours."

———

Judge Wesley is sitting by himself on one side of a small table inside an Interrogation Room at C.I.D. headquarters.

On the other side of the one-way mirror, in the Observation Room next door, the chief is schooling detectives Bishop and Chase on the best way to handle the upcoming interrogation.

Back against the wall, trying to be as inconspicuous as possible, my new partner-in-crime and I are observing everything going on around us.

A light tap on the door.

The chief opens the door a crack.

"He's here."

The chief slips out, closes the door.

Two minutes pass.

The door to the Interrogation Room opens. Ruth and I move closer to the window. We see the chief enter with another man, mid-50s, shirt and tie, carrying a briefcase.

The judge stands right up. Shakes the man's hand. "Thanks for coming, Stanley."

"Not a problem, Winston. What's this all about?"

"You'll find out momentarily," the chief says. "Detectives Bishop and Chase will be here shortly to fill in the details."

"Don't we get a private room," the man says, "where we can have a brief meeting?"

"Sorry, counselor," the chiefs says. "You're going to have to do that on your own time. This is my time."

The chief backs out, shuts the door.

The judge and the man exchange questioning glances. But they sit down without saying a word to each other.

—

Two minutes later.

Detectives Bishop and Chase enter the Interrogation Room.

The judge and his lawyer are seated next to each other. The lawyer's briefcase sits on the table, unopened.

"I'm Det. Bishop." She presents her credentials. "And this is my partner Det. Chase."

Det. Chase flashes his badge.

Both detectives remain standing.

"And you are who, sir?" she asks.

"Stanley Walsh," the man says. "I represent Judge Wesley."

"Thank you, sir," she says. "And to bring you up to speed, sir, Det. Chase already read the Miranda Rights to Judge Wesley. He declined to speak to us until you arrived."

"I see," the lawyer says. "Could you possibly be insinuating that Judge Wesley is under arrest."

"I'm not insinuating anything sir," she says. "I'm telling you flat out that Judge Wesley is already under arrest."

"This is all preposterous," the judge says.

The lawyer turns his head toward his client. "Stay calm, Winston. Let me do the talking."

"Whatever you say."

"Please, detective," the lawyer says, "Be so kind as to inform me of the charges against my client."

"We're looking at Homicide One for starters."

The judge wants to say something, but holds his tongue.

"Surely you jest, detective," the lawyer says.

"Not in the least." Det. Bishop sits down across from them. "In fact, now that you're here, we're ready to take Judge Wesley's statement."

"This is crazy." The judge sounds convincing.

"Please, Winston," the lawyer says. "Let me handle this." He looks Det. Bishop in the eye. "Judge Wesley will not be making a statement at this time."

"No problem," she says. "Donald."

Det. Chase opens the door, steps outside. The door closes. The door opens seconds later, Det. Chase returns carrying a laptop. Places it on the table.

Det. Bishop opens the laptop, punches a few keys. Turns it around so everyone can see. Starts the digital video I reproduced from Ruth's floppy.

They're looking at the landing outside the dead stripper's apartment. The door opens, and here comes Judge Wesley.

Det. Bishop pauses the video. "I believe we all know who that is."

She restarts the video.

The judge walks up to the dead stripper's apartment. Taps on the door once. The door opens a moment later.

Det. Bishop pauses the video. "The female is Miss Rita Forsythe."

She restarts the video again.

The judge steps inside the apartment, the door closes.

She stops the video. "Miss Forsythe was found dead the next day, Mr. Walsh, the victim of a manual strangulation. Later in the video we have Judge Wesley leaving the victim's apartment. The time stamps on his entry and departure overlap the time of the victim's death."

"Now," Det. Chase says, "about that statement."

CHAPTER 36

Shamrocks, leprechauns, and three-leaf clovers decorate the Broadway. The bar's decorated for St. Patrick's Day, but a perfect mood-setter for our celebration.

And the gang's all here.

My Friend and Jess. Plus Jess got Margo to tag along. Bernie and Roy. Ruth and Denny, the manager at Media Station. Farrah and Candi from Babes in Toyland. Chief George, and detectives Bishop and Chase.

Suddenly we're allies with C.I.D. instead of adversaries.

But we didn't invite the district attorney or his chief prosecutor. We tried to contact Dr. Nakamura and Agent Santangelo, but couldn't reach them. We wanted to invite the judges from my arraignment and preliminary hearing, but Bernie said it was inappropriate for them to attend.

We invited Sam Cohen and Sal the bouncer. Sam was too busy. Sal declined. Guess some hard feelings still exist.

Tony set up more tables in the alcove. Prepared an awesome buffet and supplied two cases of champagne.

—

Half an hour into our celebration.

"If it weren't for Ruth here," putting my arm around her shoulder, "I'd still be a murder suspect."

She gets a well-deserved ovation, smiles.

"Don't forget the part you played," Bernie says.

Another ovation. My turn to smile.

"How'd you get the judge to confess?" Roy asks Det. Bishop.

"He started to weaken," she says, "after he saw Ruth's video showing him entering and leaving Miss Forsythe's apartment. Then we showed him the video we got from Denny here."

Denny smiles.

"There was the judge," she says, "entering Miss Forsythe's building. Plus we told him that Mr. Piasecki–"

"You can call me Steve."

She smiles. "We told him Steve identified his car. Plus we seized the judge's phone, and his call history listed dozens of calls to Miss Forsythe, including one shortly before she was murdered. So he broke down and actually started crying."

"Like a pussy," Ruth says.

Everyone laughs.

"For sure," Det. Bishop says. "His lawyer tried to intervene, but the party was over."

"Did he say why he did it?" Bernie asks.

"She was blackmailing him," Det. Chase says, "about his sexual improprieties with her. It was getting more and more expensive to keep her quiet. So he went there to try to pay her off and end it. But she wouldn't give in."

"But what about the bathtub scene?" Roy says. "Did he do all that himself?"

"He did," Det. Chase says. "She was getting ready to take a bath when he got there. The drugs were already laid out in the bathroom. After he strangled her, all he had to do was take off her robe, lay her out in the bathtub, and dick around with the drugs."

"But," Det. Bishop says, "he made a mistake when he forgot to remove her jewelry. That created our suspicion from the beginning."

"But you thought I did it," I say.

"Yes, we did," Det. Bishop says. "Right up until you showed up with the video."

"What was your trigger?" Bernie asks me.

"I finally remembered," I say, "something she told me about a nosey neighbor and her camera."

Ruth smiles.

"So I took a chance," I say. "It took some convincing, but Ruth finally let me in her apartment and, praise the lord, she still had the video."

"And the rest, as they say," the chief says, "is history."

"How is it," Roy asks the chief," that you let these two tag along to watch?"

"They drove a hard bargain," the chief says. "They weren't going to share the video if we didn't let them observe. Steve said there was no way we'd ever find it. And we believed him."

—

A lot of mingling and getting to know each other follows.

My Friend and Margo.

Det. Chase and Denny with Farrah and Candi.

Roy and Det. Bishop.

Bernie and the chief.

Last but not least, Jess and me.

And it's a double celebration for me. After servicing Jess this morning, I checked my email. Got one from Rose Goldenberg. She purchased my story. Excalibur will publish "A Taste for Revenge" in its July edition.

But one thing's still bugging me. Wish there was some way to track down the drug cartel.

THE END

Don't miss out!

Visit the website below and you can sign up to receive emails whenever Barry Bowe publishes a new book. There's no charge and no obligation.

https://books2read.com/r/B-A-OEZJ-CQSDB

BOOKS2READ

Connecting independent readers to independent writers.

About the Author

A little more than 30 years ago Barry was teaching algebra, geometry, and trigonometry at a private school on the island of St. Croix. He was also taking correspondence courses about learning how to write.

Prior to that he was a successful sales manager in Philadelphia who always dreamed of becoming an author.

Three years later Warner Books published his first book – Born to Be Wild – a classic true-crime saga about outlaw motorcycle gangs. Bastei Verlag translated the book into German, published it under the title Der Wilde. Born to Be Wild became a Main Selection of the Doubleday Book-of-the-Month Club – and it's still selling today.

He also wrote more than 100 true murder stories for the True Detective Group of magazines. And he was the first sportswriter to put the name of NBA Hall of Famer Tim Duncan on the sports page.

Barry now writes crime fiction.

Read more at https://mycrimepays.com/.

9 798201 415471